COMPANION READER VOLUME II
TEN MORE CHRISTMAS STORIES

plus <u>TWO CHRISTMAS CLASSICS:</u>
Yes, Virginia, There Is A Santa Claus
'Twas The Night Before Christmas

SAN 299-8025

Published by *Gramma Books Publishing Co.*
Box 400
Oden, Michigan 49764
Web Site: www.grammabooks.com

Publisher's Cataloging-in-Publication
(*Provided by Quality Books, Inc.*)

McTaggart, William, R.
      Companion reader Volume II, Ten more Christmas stories ; plus, Two Christmas
classics / stories by William R. McTaggart ; illustrations by Eugene J. Hibbard. -- 1st ed.
      p.   cm.
      Includes bibliographical references.
      SUMMARY : Original values-oriented children's stories about Santa Claus and the
Christmas spirit, with two traditional pieces appended.
      CONTENTS : Yes, Virginia, there is a Santa Claus -- 'Twas the night before Christmas.
ISBN: 0-9669285-0-4

      1. Christmas stories, American.   2. Santa Claus -- Juvenile literature.   3. Children's stories.
I. Hibbard, Eugene J., ill.   II. Title.   III. Title : Ten more Christmas stories

PZ7.M478836Co 1999   [Fic]
                              QBI99-23

Printed in the United States of America

10   9   8   7   6   5   4   3   2   1

COMPANION READER VOLUME II
TEN MORE CHRISTMAS STORIES
plus TWO CHRISTMAS CLASSICS:
Yes, Virginia, There Is A Santa Claus
'Twas The Night Before Christmas

Stories by: **William R. McTaggart**

Illustrations by: **Eugene J. Hibbard**

Dedicated to those enduring precepts which will guide us toward happy and fulfilling lives:

HONESTY, COURAGE, RESPONSIBILITY, LOYALTY, AND COMPASSION FOR OTHERS

And to the parents and grandparents who do their best to instill those virtues in their children and grandchildren.

CONTENTS

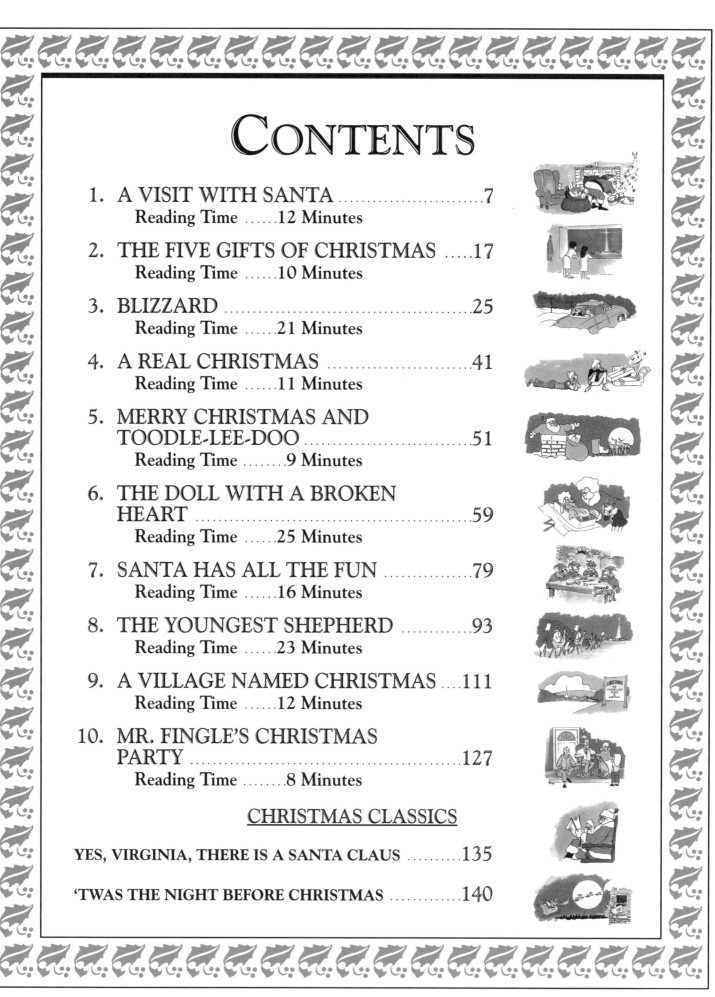

A VISIT WITH SANTA

Bobby laid his head on his pillow. This was Christmas Eve and he was too excited to sleep, but morning would come early. The McGregor family had returned from the Christmas Eve services at their church only a few minutes earlier. After putting out a glass of milk and a plate of cookies for Santa, it was almost nine o'clock. This was an hour later than Bobby's usual bedtime. Tomorrow morning he would be up at six o'clock with his little brother, Jimmie, and sister, Elizabeth, racing downstairs to their presents under the Christmas tree. Bobby was six, Jimmie was two years younger, and Beth was almost three.

As Bobby lay in bed he thought about tomorrow. He had sent a letter to Santa asking for a new bike, an electronic baseball game, and a bell for the handlebar of the bike. Bobby's mother had taken the letter to the post office to make sure it would be mailed to Santa's correct address. His mother had explained Santa's address changed every year, but the people at the post office kept track of those things and they would know Santa's new address.

Bobby's mother did not know what Bobby had asked Santa in the letter. No one knew. And no one but Santa would find out. Bobby's father had explained to the whole family at dinner two weeks ago it was against the law to open anyone else's mail, so the only one who would see Bobby's letter would be Santa. Bobby put a stamp on the letter and sealed it himself.

Bobby had included the list of presents his little brother and sister wanted Santa to bring them. Bobby wanted to make sure Santa knew what his little brother and sister wanted for Christmas. It was a puzzle how Santa could know what every kid in the world wanted for Christmas. Bobby knew there were over a thousand kids in the world, maybe thousands and thousands, when you included all the kids in China. It was a mystery how Santa could keep track of what all those kids wanted for Christmas, even if he did have elves to help him make the toys and keep things straight in Santa's Present Book.

Bobby's father had told Bobby that Santa had a book called a "Present Book" in which he kept track of what every kid wanted for Christmas. His father explained that Santa's biggest problem was with kids who changed their minds only a week before Christmas, when it was too late to have the elves make a new present. But that wasn't the half of it. Besides keeping track of the presents, Santa had to keep a record of whether the children had been good or bad. Everyone knows that kids who have been bad during the year might not get anything at all on Christmas. Keeping track of everything was a puzzle all right.

With all those questions whirling around in his head, Bobby thought he would never get to sleep. But he did -- that is until he was awakened about midnight by the clatter of hoofs on the roof. He sat up in bed. He definitely had heard something making a noise on the roof above him. He jumped out of bed and ran to the window, but he could not see what was on the roof. If it was Santa, maybe he could catch him downstairs in their living room bringing the presents. He ran downstairs. Sure enough, there was Santa putting Christmas packages under their Christmas tree.

Bobby didn't know what to do. His friends in school had told him that if anyone ever caught Santa delivering Christmas presents Santa might disappear right before their eyes, taking all the presents with him. It was a very dangerous thing to do -- catching Santa delivering presents. Bobby decided he better stand very still and not say a word.

He watched as Santa looked at a little book he held in his hand and then reached into his bag to lift out a present to place under the tree. Santa did not look up and could not have known Bobby was quietly watching him. Bobby had not made a sound -- but Santa knew. Without even turning around Santa said, "Hello, Bobby. Did I wake you up?"

"I, I, I heard your reindeer on the roof," Bobby stammered. "But it's O.K. I don't want to scare you or anything. Please don't disappear in a poof."

"Oh, don't worry, Bobby. I won't disappear. I haven't had my milk and cookies you and your brother and little sister put out for me by the fireplace. Mind if I sit down a bit and drink my milk?"

"No, that's O.K.," Bobby replied. "We wanted you to have them. The cookies are brownies my mother made. I hope you like them."

"Well, I'll like them for sure. You tell your mother that brownies are my favorite. And my reindeer like them too. Mind if I take a couple up to my reindeer on my way out?"

"No, that's O.K. too," Bobby said. "Can I ask you a question while you are drinking your milk?"

"Sure. Go right ahead. You want to know how I keep everything straight, don't you? How I remember what every little boy and girl wants to get for Christmas, and who has been good and who has been bad, right?"

"That's right. But how did you know that's what I have been wondering?"

Santa laughed. It was a deep, belly shaking laugh. "Oh, I know everything," he chuckled. "But, that's a good question, right enough," Santa said. "You're a bright young man for thinking of that. I like children who ask lots of questions. Tells me you're thinking, using your head.

"To tell the truth -- and that's a good thing too -- telling the truth. To tell the truth, without my little book I wouldn't be able to remember what child was supposed to get what present. My helpers keep the books. Without my helpers no one would ever get the right presents. Come on over here and let me show you."

Santa was sitting on the hearth next to the fireplace, drinking his milk. He put the milk glass down and moved over a bit, to make room for Bobby to sit down alongside him.

Bobby was pretty nervous. He sure didn't want to scare Santa away, but Santa seemed so friendly. Bobby walked across the room from where he had been standing and sat down next to him. Santa reached into his pocket and pulled out a little black leather book. Each page had a different letter of the alphabet -- A, B, C, all the way up to Z. Santa opened the book to the page marked M and pointed his pudgy finger at a name written in the book in green ink -- McGregor -- Bobby, Jimmie, and Elizabeth. That was Bobby's last name -- McGregor.

"See, right there," Santa said. "This is the book for the children on your block. I've already dropped off the presents to all the other children on your block. There's your name -- Bobby, your brother, Jimmie, and your little sister, Elizabeth. And see, right alongside it tells me what presents each of you want. And it's all written in green ink."

"What's that mean -- green ink?" Bobby asked.

"Oh, that means each of you has been mostly good all year. If it had been written in red ink that would mean you had been bad. Here, I'll show you." Santa turned the page of the book. "There, see that?" He pointed at a name on the page marked with a B. BLICKENSTUFF, Bradley. It had been written in red ink.

"Why, I know Brad Blickenstuff," Bobby said. "He lives just down the block, on the other side of the street. He catches raccoons and things in traps."

"Yes," Santa said sadly. "That's why his name is written in red. He almost didn't get a present this year. But later on it was reported that he feeds the birds. When we checked up on him, we found the raccoons were stealing the food Bradley put out for the birds. That is why he caught the raccoons and moved them out to the woods where they could live on wild berries, instead of eating the bird food Bradley put out. He didn't hurt the raccoons -- just caught them in live traps and moved them. Turns out Bradley is a good kid after all. But it was a close call. We've got our eye on him."

"How do you tell whether a kid's name will be written in green or in red?" Bobby asked.

"Well," Santa said, with a twinkle in his eye, "we add it up. All the good things and all the bad things, all year long. If the good things add up to more than the bad things, then we put your name in the book with green ink. If the bad things you did are more than the good things, then it's going to be red ink. That's bad news -- you betcha."

"I sure was glad to see my name in green ink. I was worried because I called Stanley Stankey a bad name once."

"Oh, I know all about that." Santa smiled as he finished off the glass of milk and took a bite of a cookie. "Called him 'Stinky Stankey', didn't you? Well that wasn't a nice thing to do. Stanley is very sensitive about his name. Doesn't like to be called 'Stinky'. We should always try to remember how other people feel and do our best not to hurt their feelings. But, as I said, we add it all up. You did a lot of good things too. Like you helped old Mrs. Lucken carry her packages out to her car. And you took out the garbage every week all year long -- except for the one week when you forgot. And you were nice to your brother and little sister. Those things add up. Got your name written in green sure enough."

Santa reached out to the cookie plate and took the three remaining cookies. He stuffed them into the pocket of his red coat. "These are for my reindeer," he said with a smile. Then without another word, Santa picked up his toy bag, laid his finger alongside his nose, mumbled a word Bobby could not hear, and shot up the chimney as quick as a wink.

That was the last Bobby ever saw of Santa Claus. He did not wake up until six thirty the next morning, which was a half hour later than he had planned to wake up when he went to bed the night before. Maybe that was because he didn't get to bed until an hour later than his usual bedtime. Or maybe he slept later because of the time he had been up talking to Santa during the night. It seemed so real. Probably just a dream. Still -- a marvelous dream.

Time to open presents. Bobby reached across to Jimmie's bed, to shake the bed to awaken his little brother. They both leaped out of bed and ran to Elizabeth's room, to get her up too. The three of them tore downstairs to light up the Christmas tree and find their presents. Santa certainly had been here during the night. The glass of milk they left for Santa was empty and all the cookies were gone. Only a crumb or two remained on the plate.

Every present Bobby had asked for in his letter to Santa was there, including the ones he had told Santa his brother and sister wanted. It was a splendid Christmas. Bobby's dream seemed so real it was easy to believe it may have really happened.

At breakfast that morning, when the whole family sat down around the dining room table, Bobby's father asked, "Well, children, did each of you get the presents you were hoping for?"

"Oh, yes," they replied together. "It's a wonderful Christmas."

"I had a fantastic dream," Bobby said. "I heard Santa's reindeer on the roof. It woke me up and I went downstairs to see if he was here. And, he was. He was putting our presents under the tree. I was real quiet but he knew I was watching him, and he said hello to me. I talked to him and he told me how he keeps records of what everybody does -- good kids and bad kids. Green ink is for good kids. Red ink is for bad kids. But they add it all up and put it in a little black book. Santa showed me the book for the kids on our block."

"Wow," said Jimmie. "That's awesome!"

"Was it a real dream, Bobby?" Elizabeth asked.

"Well, it sure seemed real," Bobby said.

"By the way," father asked, "did any of you lose this little leather book I found this morning on the floor next to the fireplace? It has the names of all the children in our block."

"Why that's Santa's little black book!" Bobby exclaimed.

"Oh. Oh," Jimmie said.

"Oh. Oh," little Elizabeth said.

The End

THE FIVE GIFTS OF CHRISTMAS

Abrilliant light pierced the darkness and fell upon the sleeping eyes of Jacob. Awakened by the brightness, Jacob pulled aside the robe under which he slept and crept to the window of his home in Bethlehem. He saw an unusually dazzling star in the heavens above. Through a parting in the clouds, the star cast its shimmering light into Jacob's bedroom window and across the room to the straw bed where Jacob had been sleeping. Jacob gazed at the star. He was fascinated by the beam of light that fell upon his face.

"What is it?" asked a voice beside him. The voice belonged to Sarah, Jacob's younger sister. She too had been awakened by the bright light.

"I have never seen a star so bright," Jacob replied. "And look, the light is moving down the street, toward the Inn." A pencil of light broke through an opening in a cloud. As a tiny breath of air moved the cloud through the sky, the finger of light slowly traced a path along the cobblestone street in front of their house, in the direction of the Inn at the end of the street.

There had hardly been a whisper of air, and now there was none at all. The cloud did not move and the light from the star seemed fixed upon the Inn -- or rather upon the stable at the back of the Inn, casting a radiance nearly as bright as day.

Jacob remained captivated by the sight, for he had never seen anything like it in all of his ten years. His sister, too, was entranced, and somewhat afraid, for she was only seven years old. The night air was cold. Both children shivered in the coolness as they stood by the open window. They waited and they watched, yet the light remained firmly in place pointing its ray at the stable.

"Let us go see," Jacob said. "It is only down the street."

"Is it an omen?" Sarah asked, for these were ancient days. Science was young and there were many things people did not understand. Things they did not understand they often called omens or signs from Heaven of things to come.

"I do not know," Jacob said, "but I believe we must find out. Something of greatness must be happening."

"Aren't you afraid?" Sarah asked.

"There is nothing to be afraid of, little sister. It is only a light. A light cannot hurt us. The sun is a light, but it does not hurt us, does it?"

"Can I hold your hand then, Jacob?" Sarah asked.

"If it will make you feel better, of course you can," Jacob said, reaching out to his sister. "But it is cold outside. We must get our cloaks."

They did not wish to awaken their parents so they crept quietly to the door by the street. Their woolen cloaks hung on pegs next to the door. Each child in the family had his own peg on the wall upon which hung their cloaks. Jacob and Sarah wrapped their cloaks about themselves. Although the cloaks were worn they were warm and kept out the cold night air. They quietly lifted the latch on the door and stepped into the street with hardly a sound. The light from the star remained fixed upon the stable behind the Inn.

Sarah clung to her brother's hand as they walked down the empty street. She was trying very hard not to be afraid. She had never been out this late at night before, and except for the light from the star at the end of the street it was dark. They saw no one else on the street as they approached the Inn. Jacob and Sarah reached the stable without trouble. The light from the star shone inside the entrance to the stable, lighting the interior, just as it had lit their bedroom. They could see a man and woman, strangers to the village, standing beside a manger in the stable. Then they heard a sound. The sound of a baby. The child was crying.

Jacob did not know what to do. He felt they were intruding upon the privacy of others, yet somehow he was drawn to the strangers and to the baby. But Sarah, who loved babies more than anything, lost all the fear she had earlier. She wanted to see the baby and maybe hold it if she could. Sarah still held her brother's hand. She pulled him toward the strangers. As they got closer the children could see the woman was standing beside a tiny baby lying upon a bed of straw.

No one said anything, neither the strangers nor Jacob or Sarah. The mother was trying to shelter the baby from the cold but there were no blankets. It was obvious the baby was cold, for it was whimpering and in distress.

Sarah, though only seven, could tell the child was in want, for she had cared for two younger sisters and knew much about the needs of infants. She turned to Jacob. "The little baby is cold, Jacob."

"Yes," Jacob said, "we must help them." With those words Jacob removed his woolen cloak and gently covered the baby. "I am afraid my cloak is well worn and has a tear but it is warm and will help the baby."

The man smiled in appreciation and carefully swaddled the baby in Jacob's woolen cloak. The infant was comforted and soon drifted off into sleep. The gift of Jacob's cloak was the FIRST GIFT OF CHRISTMAS.

The man spoke. "Thank you. We are strangers to your town of Bethlehem and we did not know what to do. This is my wife, Mary, and I am Joseph. The baby is our first born. We have decided to call him Jesus. We wished to stay in the Inn but they told us there was no room and sent us to their stable. We have no blankets and we were most worried for the safety of our child. The infant will be warm and comfortable now. The gift of your cloak was a most loving thing to do. But now we worry for you. You have only your nightclothes, and it is cold."

Jacob's young sister, Sarah, spoke up. "We will be all right for I have my own cloak, which I will share with my brother." And with those words Sarah wrapped half of her cloak around her brother's shoulders. That was the SECOND GIFT OF CHRISTMAS.

The two children bade Mary and Joseph good night and left to return to their home. They walked close to each other, sharing the warmth of Sarah's cloak.

They went quietly into their house. But their mother, having awakened a few minutes earlier, had arisen from her own bed and was worriedly searching the house for the two children.

"What in the world are you doing out in the cold, children?" Mother said. "And where is your cloak, Jacob? You must be freezing."

"Sarah shared her cloak with me, Mother, though I did not need it. I feel very warm. We found a little baby that was cold and needed a cover. I gave the child my cloak."

Just then Jacob's father walked into the room. He had heard them talking. He had a stern look on his face. "You say you gave your cloak away to a baby? What kind of parents do not have a blanket for their own child? Your mother and I work very hard for our clothing. We cannot go around giving everything away. Who were these people?"

"They were strangers to the village, Father," Jacob said. "They said their names were Joseph and Mary. The child was a newborn baby. They named him Jesus. I think they may have been very poor. They were turned away by the Inn. We found them in the stable behind the Inn, where the light from the star took us. They were doing their best trying to keep the baby warm, but Sarah and I knew the baby was cold and needed help. That is why I gave them my cloak. I hope you and Mother will forgive me."

Jacob's father and mother stared at their children. Then the parents turned to each other. Tears came into their eyes. They knew Jacob and Sarah were good children doing their best to help those who needed it. They reached out their arms to each other and to the children. Holding them all, Father said, "You did as we would do ourselves, and as we have tried to teach you. Though you now have no cloak to keep you warm, what you did was done out of concern for the needs of others, not through carelessness. You are forgiven, Jacob."

Forgiveness in return for kindness was the THIRD GIFT OF CHRISTMAS.

Then Sarah turned to hang up her cloak on her wooden peg by the door.

"Look, Jacob!" Sarah exclaimed. "There is a cloak on your peg. It is brand new and of the finest wool. How could that happen?"

Jacob ran to the cloak. He lifted it from his peg, slipped his arms into the sleeves, and wrapped it around him. It fit perfectly.

"It is a miracle!" Jacob laughed joyfully. "A gift most needed from a benefactor unknown."

And that was the FOURTH GIFT OF CHRISTMAS.

They were all amazed.

"Where in the world do you suppose Jacob's new cloak came from?" Jacob's father asked. "How can we explain such wonders?"

Then Jacob's mother spoke, "I believe it must be the fruit of Love," she said. "Only Love can work such miracles."

The truth Jacob and Sarah learned that night was of the astonishing magic of Love given from the heart without expectation of reward. It was extraordinary knowledge which guided Jacob and Sarah throughout their whole lives. It brought joy and friendship to all they met -- and to themselves -- most of all. The wisdom Jacob and Sarah acquired that Night of The Star was the FIFTH GIFT OF CHRISTMAS.

The End

BLIZZARD

"Where are you planning to go lady?" the rental car agent asked my mother.

"We are on our way to my parent's farm," she replied. "They live near Maple City."

"That's a forty-mile trip. You planning on making the trip in this weather, with those kids?" the rental agent asked.

There were three of us plus my mother. My sister, Kristen, who is seven. Bobby, our new baby, and me. I am ten. My name is Thomas. Tom for short. Well, my parents call me Tommy. I kinda wish they'd call me Tom. When they call me Tommy in front of my friends it's embarrassing.

It was Christmas Eve. We had just arrived at the northern Michigan airport from Los Angeles, where we live. This was a special trip to spend Christmas with Mom's folks at their farm. We hadn't been back to Michigan since we moved to Los Angeles three years ago. I was very excited about seeing Grandpa and Grandma for the first time in three years. And Mom had promised we could learn to ski this Christmas.

Dad couldn't come with us because he had an important meeting with his company in Los Angeles the day after Christmas. But he would join us in a couple of days. We had talked about waiting and all of us coming out together, but we wanted to spend Christmas with Mom's folks at the farm. There isn't any snow in Los Angeles, and it doesn't seem like a real Christmas without snow. Besides you can't ski without snow. There is plenty of snow in northern Michigan.

A little snow didn't bother us. My sister, Kristen, and I had been born in Michigan. We lived there until Dad's company transferred him to southern California. Bobby, our baby brother, is two years old. He has never seen snow before, but he is a good baby and will like it.

"Real mean storm coming in from the north," the rental car agent said. "The roads may be tough to navigate." You could see he was worried for Mom and us kids.

"I'm afraid we don't have much choice," Mother replied. "We have no place else to stay. We'll just have to take our chances."

"Well, good luck," the agent said as he went to get the car from the parking lot.

We waited by our stuff at the baggage gate, while the attendant drove the car up to the door. We had a lot of baggage to load including all the Christmas presents we had brought from home. I could tell Mom was a little nervous about the drive from the airport to the farm. There was six inches of snow on the ground and more was falling every minute. If the wind picked up it could be a real blizzard. We had seen northern Michigan blizzards before. Can't see your hand in front of your face in a real one. They were worse at night, and it was already plenty dark. Our plane had not landed until ten o'clock.

The snowplows were busy and the main roads were pretty much cleared off. Only the last half-mile to the farm might be a little tough. They didn't usually plow the road in front of the farm until two or three days after a big storm. And this looked like a big one. I was excited. Nothing like sitting in front of a roaring fire in Grandpa's farmhouse with the wind whistling and snow blowing outside.

We climbed in the car and fastened our seat belts. Bobby was in the backseat in his car carrier. "We'll be all right," Mother said. "It's only forty miles and the snowplows do a good job of keeping the roads clear up here." I think she was trying to reassure herself as much as the rest of us. As we headed toward Maple City the snow began falling faster. I was riding in the front passenger seat, keeping an eye out ahead. It was getting harder and harder to see. It was pitch dark and there was hardly any traffic on the road since it was Christmas Eve. Most everyone was safely home by now.

By the time we got to Maple City we could barely see fifty feet in front of us. Mother decided we had better call ahead to her parents, to let them know we were on our way and only five miles from the farm. We pulled up in front of a pay telephone and Mother got out to make the call. When she returned she looked worried.

"What's up?" I asked.

"Well, your grandparents are happy to hear we got to Maple City, but they are worried about the drifting snow. They say the snowplows have quit for the night because of high winds and drifting snow. Grandpa and Grandma are worried we may have trouble getting out to the farm. They want us to try to find a place to stay in town and wait until morning."

"Gee," I said. "I don't want to hang around in town. It's only a couple of miles to the farm. Can't we keep going? Besides, where will we find a place to stay this late at night on Christmas Eve? Everything looks closed up." We probably could have found a motel all right. I just wanted to see Grandpa and Grandma.

"You want to try it, Tommy?" Mother said. "Maybe we should call Grandpa and Grandma and let them know we are coming. They probably think we'll stay in town 'till morning, when the roads are cleared."

I liked it when Mom treated me like a grownup, asking me what I thought; even if she still called me Tommy. "Naw," I said, "let's keep going. The longer we wait, the deeper the snow is getting." It was easy for me to say. I wasn't doing the driving.

She started the car and we headed out of town. That was a mistake. My fault, too. We should have called Grandpa to let him know we were still on the road and not holed up back in town. Once we left town there was no way we could call him.

We managed the winding road up the hill out of town, but when we reached the top of the hill we were no longer sheltered by the trees. The wind roared down upon us with a fury I had never seen. It was a blinding blizzard. We could not even see the front end of the car, and the glare from the headlights against the driving snow seemed to make it worse. Mother was leaning forward, striving to see what was ahead. I, too, had my face close to the windshield, trying to make out the roadway beneath the drifting snow. The snow was so deep on the road it was impossible to turn around. We had no choice except to keep going.

By some miracle we reached the corner where the road to the farm intersects the road from town. We were only a half-mile from the farm. There were no houses between here and the farm. We had passed the last farmhouse a mile back.

Right then I sure wished I had not told Mom to keep going when we were back in town. If I had kept my big mouth shut we would be warm and safe for the night in a motel. It was too late to worry about that now.

As we turned the corner heading for the farm, we could see a big snowdrift covering the road. Mother accelerated, trying to bust through the drift. But that was the end. The front of the car plowed into the hard-packed snowdrift, and the car was lifted off the road. Our wheels were no longer in contact with the surface of the road. We could not back up and we could not go forward. We were stuck, and stuck good.

My little sister in the backseat had been quiet since we left Maple City, but now she began to cry. Who could blame her? We were in big trouble and we all knew it. Then the baby began to cry too. Mother and I looked at each other. Neither of us said a word.

"Unhook the baby's car seat, Susan, and hand him to me." That would keep Susan busy for a bit. "Tommy, see if you can get your door open and make it back to the trunk. Bring up all the Christmas presents."

"You want me to bring the presents up here? Are we going to have Christmas in the car?" It seemed funny. Here we were about to die of freezing and Mother was thinking of opening presents. Mother could see the humor in it and she giggled along with me.

"What's so funny?" Susan asked. It didn't seem funny to her. Susan had handed the baby to Mother and Bobby stopped crying once he was cradled in Mother's arms. The car was still warm and comfortable.

"It's your strange brother," Mother said, replying to Susan's question. "He thinks everything is funny. Probably would laugh hanging to the side of a sinking ship in the ocean."

Susan giggled at that. Nobody in this family would go down without a fight.

I pushed the door open through the snow piled against the side of the car. Luckily I had worn my heavy hiking boots. Mother turned off the engine and handed me the keys to the trunk. I waded through the snow to the rear of the car, brushed the snow off the trunk, and opened it. I found the presents and carried them back to the car. I climbed back inside and handed the keys to my mother. She started the car and turned up the heater, in an effort to replace the heat we had lost while I retrieved the presents.

"Early Christmas kids," Mother said, handing Susan and me large boxes that were gaily wrapped in Christmas paper. We eagerly tore the wrapping from our presents. Inside the boxes were complete ski outfits for each of us -- parkas, heavy ski pants, and insulated after-ski boots.

"Put them on," Mother said. "They ought to keep you good and warm." Bobby was snuggled in his blanket. He was warm and comfortable in Mother's arms.

"Wow," I said, as I pulled on the ski clothes over my regular clothes. "These are neat, Mom. Thanks a lot."

"You're welcome," Mom said. "You can tell all your friends we decided to have Christmas in the car on Christmas Eve in the middle of a blizzard."

We all laughed, but then fell silent, as we stared at the blackness outside and listened to the wind as it shook the car in its fury. No one said a word but you could tell we were plenty scared. No one would be fool enough to be out in a night like this, and there wasn't any hope of someone coming to rescue us. It looked like we might freeze to death, only a half-mile from our destination. We couldn't expect Grandpa to come looking for us. He thought we were safe for the night in a comfortable motel back in town.

"Well, now what?" Mother said, staring out the windshield at the darkness.

"I read that you shouldn't keep the car running if you get stuck in snow," I said. "The fumes can kill you if the exhaust pipe gets buried in the snow."

"I read that too," Mother replied, switching off the engine. "Maybe we can run it a little bit from time to time, as long as we make sure the snow hasn't covered the exhaust pipe." It seemed colder already with the engine off. The car shook as the winter wind pounded against it. Susan and I pulled on our new parkas. Mother showed us how the hoods pulled up over our heads, leaving only our noses out. We sat quietly for several minutes, listening to the howling wind. No one said a word.

"Well, kids," Mother broke the silence. "I don't think we can survive the night if we sit here. Someone is going to have to hike the half-mile to Dad's farmhouse and bring him back here to help."

"I'm ready, Mom," I said. I knew it was up to me. Mother couldn't leave the baby.

"I can go along to help," Susan said.

"That's very brave of you, Susan," Mother replied, "but I need you here to help care for the baby."

We all knew the truth. There was only one person who could rescue us -- me.

I pulled the drawstring in the hood tight and mother tied it beneath my chin. I pulled on my new ski mittens, which had been stuffed in the pockets of the parka, and opened the door.

"Stay on the road," Mother called out as I stepped into the night. I was quickly swallowed by darkness and swirling snow. The farm was a half-mile straight ahead. I had walked on this same road with my dad twice before, in the summer when we were here three years ago. But I had never walked it by myself, and never at night in the winter in the middle of a howling blizzard. One thing was certain, I didn't have to worry about getting run over by a car. There were no cars out on a night like this. And -- no chance we might be rescued by a passing motorist.

Even though it was pitch dark with blowing snow I could still make out the telephone poles alongside the road, beckoning me in the direction of Grandpa's farm. The road was drifted over but I could follow the poles. I figured that as long as I stayed on the road I would eventually come to the farmhouse. I began trudging ahead, one step at a time.

The wind was howling straight out of the north. Wind does funny things. Sometimes the road was almost bare where the wind had swept the snow clean. Other times the snow was waist deep where a row of trees or a bank of earth on the upwind side of the road caused the wind to swirl around and drop its load of snow on the road.

After fighting my way through deep snowdrifts I discovered that when there was a steep bank of earth or row of trees on the upwind side of the road I should keep as far downwind from the bank as possible. There the snow was not drifted so deep. But I always made sure I stayed on the road.

One time I wandered a little too far downwind, trying to keep out of the deep snowdrifts. I ended up sliding down into the roadside ditch. The snow was almost over my head. When I finally struggled out of that mess I promised myself to be more careful.

A half-mile is a long way in the summer. It seemed almost impossible to a ten-year-old kid floundering through snowdrifts in the dark of night. But I knew it was up to me. My whole family depended on me. I would keep going until I reached the farm -- or bust in the tryin'.

After what seemed half the night had passed I was getting tired from fighting my way against the wind and through the drifts. I began to wonder if I might have wandered off the road, heading for nowhere. If I had gotten off the road in the darkness and began wandering across the open fields, there would be no way anyone would find me until next spring.

Suddenly the wind and the blowing snow cleared a bit. Through the darkness I could see a light ahead. It had to be Grandpa's farm. I fought my way up the driveway and pounded on the door. I had made it.

The door opened. Grandma threw up her hands and shouted with joy. "They're here! They're here! Land sakes, child. We have been worried sick. We called all the motels in town and they said you hadn't checked in anywhere."

Grandpa came running. "Where are the others, Tommy?"

"We have to go get them, Grandpa. They're at the turn in the road. The car is stuck. I had to come get you."

"Well, come on in and stand up by the fire. Take the chill off your bones. Like to freeze to death out in this kind of weather. By golly how you've grown. Man-size already. I'll go hitch up the sleigh."

Grandpa hurriedly pulled on a heavy sweater, wrapped a woolen scarf around his neck, and climbed into his winter work pants and coveralls. "Come on out to the barn and help," he said. "We'll put old Pat and Mike to work. They could use the exercise." Pat and Mike were Grandpa's two workhorses.

"Wait just a minute you two," Grandma said. "Let me get some of this hot chocolate down your gullet. You must be freezing somethin' fierce."

"Naw, I'm fine, Grandma. See my new ski clothes. They're my Christmas present. Susan got some too. We weren't supposed to get them until tomorrow, but Mom decided tonight was a good time to put them on. I'm warm as toast. Mom and Dad promised we could learn to ski this Christmas."

"Well, land sakes. That's all I can say. Gracious to glory. Are they all right? Are they still in the car? Not out in the snow? And the baby. Is the baby all right?"

"I'm sure they are all okay, Grandma. They were nice and warm when I left, and that wasn't too long ago, even though it seemed like forever. Mom planned on running the car a little bit at a time, so they could stay warm but not get monoxided. But we've got to go get them. They can't stay there all night."

"Come on, man," Grandpa said. "Let's hitch up the horses to the sleigh and get them. Can't be standin' around jawin'. There's work to be done."

Boy, did I like that. Grandpa calling me 'man' and all.

We headed for the barn. The horses whinnied their approval as Grandpa backed them out of their stalls and walked them out into the barnyard to hitch them to the sleigh. They didn't like being idle all winter and the fierce weather didn't bother them a bit. They knew Grandpa would take care of them.

"Run into the barn, Tom, and haul out a couple of bales of hay. Got to make a nice soft bed for your family."

I ran back into the barn and found the piled up bales of hay. One by one I managed to drag them out to the sleigh. Grandpa had already hitched the horses and was ready to go. We climbed on board and headed out to the road. As we drove down the driveway past the house, Grandma came running with an armload of blankets for us to take.

The horses were used to hard work and their long legs stepped right through the drifts as if they were nothing. As we approached the car Mother saw us coming and flashed the lights, showing us they were all right. Grandpa kept going until we reached the corner, where there was room to turn the sleigh around. He made the turn and pulled the sleigh alongside the car. "Want a taxi?" Grandpa called out. "Climb aboard."

I jumped off the sleigh and carried the blankets to the car while Grandpa cut the string from the bales of hay and made a nest for everyone on the sleigh.

"Leave the car," Grandpa hollered over the roar of the wind. "We'll come get it tomorrow."

Wrapped in the blankets, everyone climbed aboard and snuggled down in the thick bed of hay. Off we went, back down the road to the farm. No one was the worse for wear. We unloaded our passengers at the kitchen door and Grandpa and I took the horses up to the barn.

There were lots of hugs and kisses all around, along with great sighs of relief. Grandma was holding her new grandchild in her arms, both of them giggling and carrying on, as if they had known each other forever. Grandmas have a way with babies.

As we sipped cups of hot chocolate Mother related the whole adventure, telling how Susan offered to go with me to find help.

Grandpa turned to Mother and said, "Well, daughter, that wasn't the smartest thing you have done in your life, you know. We thought you were going to stay in town at a nice safe motel, and not try to fight the blizzard."

It was my turn to reply. "It wasn't Mother's fault, Grandpa. It was my idea to keep going. We would have stayed in town but I wanted to get back to see you and Grandma in the worst way. I talked Mom into driving out tonight."

Grandpa looked at me for a minute, not saying a word. Finally, looking me straight in the eye, he asked, "Were you scared, Tommy?"

"Yeah, I guess I was. Especially when I fell down into the ditch. Thought I'd never get out of there."

"Well, I'm real proud of you, son," Grandpa said.

"Wasn't he brave, though?" Grandma exclaimed.

"Oh, they were all brave," Grandpa said. "Little Susan wanted to go along and help too, and she's only seven. But that's not what makes me most proud of our family. 'Course Tom was scared. Any man would be plenty scared. There was a whole lot restin' on his shoulders. Coulda' lost the whole family. A man's got to do what a man's got to do, you know.

"But best of all's the fact he showed us he's got back-bone and he's honest. Could have let his mother take the blame for being the one who should have known better. Tom didn't do that. He stepped up to his own responsibility. Told us he was the one to blame for puttin' the family in danger. Didn't hesitate a second. Now that takes a man -- a man of courage.

"Proud to have you as our grandson, Tom," Grandpa said, reaching out to shake my hand.

I never forgot that night -- called me Tom.

The End

A REAL CHRISTMAS

Only two more days until Christmas. The family was having dinner at Angelo's, a local Italian restaurant. They often ate dinner at restaurants because both father and mother worked full time. Mary's father was an engineer and her mother owned a ladies' dress shop. Both worked long hours and often there was not enough time to prepare dinner at home.

"Looking forward to Christmas, Mary?" Dad asked.

"Oh, sure," Mary replied.

"You don't sound very excited."

"Oh, it's okay, I guess."

"Last I looked," Dad said, "there was a pile of presents under the tree. Enough for an army, looks to me."

"Yeah, I guess," Mary responded.

"Something has been bothering both kids," Mary's mother said. "John isn't much more enthusiastic either." John was Mary's younger brother. He was eight years old. Mary was ten.

"How about letting us in on it?" Dad said. "Something bugging you guys?"

John spoke up. "We never have a real Christmas," he said.

"Why can't we have a real Christmas sometime? Other kids do," Mary said, looking down at her plate. It was plain to see she wasn't happy.

"Yeah," John said, "the Fairchilds have a great Christmas."

"I doubt the Fairchild children get more presents than you kids," Dad said. "You guys do pretty well, in my opinion." Dad was getting a little peeved at what he thought were two ungrateful children. "There are plenty of children who don't even have a Christmas."

Mary's face had begun to cloud up. She was close to tears. "It's not the presents, Daddy. We get too many presents. But we never have a real Christmas."

Dad turned to his wife. "Do you have any idea what they are talking about, Martha? I think I'm missing something. It's obvious the kids are upset."

"Well, I know something is bothering them, but I haven't been able to get it out of them. Anyway, I've got to get back to the store. This is our busiest time of year. Everybody wants a new dress for Christmas. Got to make hay while the sun shines."

Mother was a very good businesswoman. She operates a successful high-end clothing store, and was busy most of the year. Christmas was particularly busy and she often got home as the children were preparing for bed. The whole family was proud of mother's success, even though it took her out of the home much of the time.

"I'm afraid I've got to run," Mother said. "Why don't the rest of you take your time and have some dessert? We are going to keep the store open until ten tonight, to pick up last minute shoppers. I should be home about eleven." She picked up her purse, kissed her husband, and waved good-bye.

The rest of the family finished dinner and climbed into the car to return to their home. On the way home Dad asked, "Okay, kids, what's the deal? Something is bothering you. Let Dad in on it."

Mary replied. "It's just, just --- you and Mom get us lots of presents. More'n we deserve. But it just doesn't seem like a real Christmas. Julie Ann has a real Christmas."

"Julie Ann Fairchild?" Dad asked.

"And Donny Fairchild, too. They have a real Christmas," John added.

Nothing more was said the rest of the way home. The children's father, however, resolved to call Jim Fairchild as soon as he got home. Jim and Betty Fairchild lived down the street from the Martin family. They were all good friends.

Upon their return home the children went to their rooms to do their homework. Dad picked up the phone and dialed the Fairchild home. Jim Fairchild answered the phone.

"Jim, this is Paul Martin, down the street. Need to consult with you about what a real Christmas is. Seems Mary and John are a little upset with us for not having a real Christmas -- whatever that means. We load them up with presents every year, but that doesn't seem to be what they think a real Christmas is supposed to be. Mary tells us your children - Julie Ann and Donny - have a real Christmas. Mind clueing me in? What's a real Christmas?"

Jim Fairchild chuckled. "Sorry about that Paul. We don't mean to upset the neighbors. The kids have been talking among themselves. I overheard Julie Ann and Mary discussing Christmas a couple of days ago. Julie Ann was telling Mary what we have done for the last two Christmases. That may be what Mary means by a real Christmas."

"Well, what's that?" Paul asked.

"We open presents on Christmas day, and have the usual turkey dinner. Then the next day we pile the kids into the car and head for the mountains. We rent a cabin at a ski resort for the week after Christmas, and kind of all snuggle in together. It's the one time during the year when we all get together as a family. Got to admit we have a good time."

"Sounds like fun, all right," Paul replied, "but I don't see how we could do that. Martha's store is the busiest this time of year. And my plant has new projects they expect me to engineer in order to get into production by spring. I don't see how we could get away, for even a day or two."

"Yeah, it's a busy time of year all right," Jim replied. "We just decide to take the time off to be with the kids. Let the rest of the world complain if it wants. The kids grow up too fast as it is. Can you believe it? Julie Ann will be going to high school in another year. And Donny has only three more years before he finishes middle school. Won't be long before they're both away to college. Time flies by and all of a sudden the kids are married and gone."

"Well, I got my answer," Paul said. "I'm sure Martha won't be able to get away from her store, but what's the name of the ski resort you go to, just in case? And thanks a lot."

He wrote the name and telephone number of the ski resort on the pad of paper by the telephone and hung up. As he sat thinking, he knew there was no way he could break away from work for a whole week. And he knew Martha would not be able to leave the store either. They were both simply too busy.

Then he dialed the number of the ski resort. He could discuss it with Martha when she returned home at eleven.

On Christmas day the children had a great time opening their presents. Martha didn't have the time or energy to cook a turkey, but they picked up a pre-cooked turkey with all the fixin's at the local caterer and enjoyed dinner together at home. The children seemed to have forgotten what the Fairchild family did at Christmas.

The day after Christmas Mother didn't go to work. Neither did Dad. Instead Dad announced to the children, "Okay, kids. Get your stuff packed up. We're going to take a trip. Bring along plenty of warm clothes and some of the games you got for Christmas. We'll see if we can figure out how to play the games while were on the road."

"Where are we going, Daddy?" John asked.

"You'll see," Dad replied. "It's a secret."

The family climbed into the loaded car and they started down the road. "How can you leave your store, Mother?" Mary asked. "Won't they be busy?" Mary knew that during the week following Christmas many dresses were returned to be exchanged for different sizes or styles.

"Your Daddy convinced me there are more important things than running a business," Mother replied. Then, reaching out with her hand to caress the cheek of her husband, she said with a warm smile, "Didn't you, dear?"

As the family continued their journey the children found one of the games they had received at Christmas. It was a word game they could play as they travelled. For the first time in many months they were all together. The miles flew by as they laughed and teased each other, played games and told stories.

At noon they pulled into a McDonald's to get some lunch. John said, "Let's take lunch with us Dad. I can hardly wait to get to wherever we're going. How much longer is it going to be?"

"You'll see," Father replied. "Couple more hours should do it."

They were heading north and the snow on the ground was getting deeper. Finally, the car turned off the main highway onto a county road. A mile further they turned into a plowed drive. A sign on the drive said: "Mountain View Lodge."

"Here we are," Dad said.

"Mountain View Lodge!" Mary exclaimed. "That's where Julie Ann and her family go every Christmas. And there is their car!" she cried out.

"Look for a cabin named Moose," Dad said. "We have the Moose cabin."

"Wow!" John cried. "This is where Donny Fairchild said they were going after Christmas. They have skiing and snowshoeing and swimming in a heated pool. Everybody eats in the lodge. Wow! This is the best ever."

The car slowed to a stop in front of a log cabin with the name Moose over the door. They unloaded their suitcases and climbed the steps of the cabin. Inside they found a fireplace with a cheerful fire already burning in anticipation of their arrival.

"Where do we sleep?" John said.

"Grab one of the upper bunks, John," Dad replied. "Us old folks get to sleep in the lowers. The cabin was one large

room with four bunks on one side and a game table in the middle, in front of the fireplace. There was a single bathroom with a shower.

"Where is the kitchen, Paul?" Mother asked.

"No kitchen, Martha. Everyone eats together in the lodge. We'll eat with about ten other families. No cooking for the ladies for the whole week."

"Oh, Daddy," Mary gasped. "We are going to be here for a whole week? All together in our own cabin with our own fireplace?"

"Yep," Dad said. "Can't fight with your brother for a whole week. Not enough time. You kids will be skiing every day and at the end of the day they have an outdoor swimming pool with warm water to take the kinks out. Have to run through the snow and jump in the water real quick."

"It's Heaven," Mary said, flopping down on one of the bunks. "And Julie Ann is here too. We'll be together for a whole week."

"Wow," sighed John, hugging his mother.

For the week following Christmas the Martin family skied and swam and played games on the game table, and became re-acquainted with each other.

Mary skied with Julie Ann and John skied with his friend, Donny. They all ate together in the lodge, with ten other families. At night they were so tired from all the activities they slept as they had never slept before.

On the day before New Year's the family packed their belongings and climbed into their car to head for home. As he started the car, Father turned to Mary, "Well, Mary, how was your Christmas this year?"

"Oh, Daddy," she sighed, smiling from ear to ear, "that was a REAL Christmas."

"Delicious," said mother.

"Bucket of ice!" John exclaimed. "BIG bucket of ice."

The End

MERRY CHRISTMAS AND TOODLE-LEE-DOO

Mrs. Claus helped Santa pull on his warmest boots as he dressed for his long trip around the world on Christmas Eve.

"Now don't forget this year, Santa", she said.

"Of course, my dear," Santa replied. "I won't forget. Last year my carelessness delayed our flight for almost half an hour. Would have been a disaster if we had been unable to complete the trip before the sun came up. I lose my magic if we do not return to the North Pole before dawn. It is a long trip and we cannot lose a moment. We would not be able to deliver presents to all the boys and girls throughout the world. A terrible calamity."

"Well," said Mrs. Claus, "in your haste to deliver all the presents it's easy enough to forget. Just try to remember not to say the 'get big' word until you are out of the chimney."

"That was most embarrassing, all right," Santa chuckled. "I said the magic 'get big' word at the top of the chimney. Swelled up like a balloon and got stuck in little Susie's chimney. Most embarrassing."

"Got black soot all over your coat. Took me a week to wash it all out," said Mrs. Claus.

"Well," Santa replied, "it's not an easy job you know. Lots to remember. I have to remember all the children who have been good and all the children who have been bad. Then I have to remember what every child in the whole world wants for Christmas. That's not easy."

"Yes, dear. I know. Just try to remember not to say 'oopladoop' before you get out of the chimney and into the children's houses. You'll swell up and get stuck again."

" 'Oopladoop'!" Santa laughed. "What do you mean, 'oopladoop'? That's not the right word. The word to make me swell up is 'poopadoop'. You should know that by now. It's 'poopadoop'."

"Whatever," Mrs. Claus replied. "Here, put your arm in your coat. It's almost time to start. I can hear the reindeer stomping in the snow outside. They're all hitched up and ready to go."

"Feeling their oats, are they?" Santa said. "Well, let them wait a bit. I need a cup of hot chocolate before I head out. It's cold outside this time of year. 'Oopladoop', my word. It's a good thing you're not going along. We'd both be stuck in somebody's chimney if you said 'oopladoop' instead of 'poopadoop.'"

"Oh, 'poopadoop' yourself," Mrs. Claus said. "Here, put your scarf on. Don't want the wind blowing down your neck as you go racing across the world."

Santa wrapped the scarf around his neck, chuckling to himself. "Bet you don't remember the get small word either," he said to Mrs. Claus.

"Of course I do," Mrs. Claus replied. "It's 'papadown'. That's what it is. 'Papadown'."

"Aha!" exclaimed Santa. "'Papadown' wouldn't do anything. The get small word is 'lotsasmall'."

"Whatever," responded Mrs. Claus. "Here, put on your hat. You know there is scientific evidence that most of our body heat escapes through our heads. You'll take a chill if you don't keep your hat on. Now sit right there while I get you a cup of hot chocolate."

Just then Arthur, Santa's elf in charge of the reindeer, ran into the house. "Santa, what are you doing sitting there? The reindeer are ready to go. If you don't get started soon there won't be enough time to get all the way around the world. Some of the children may not get a present."

"Oh rattlescamp," Santa replied, somewhat put out by all the fussing. "There's plenty of time. It's going to be cold up there and it's a long trip. Mrs. Claus is making me a cup of hot chocolate. Besides, she's got me all mixed up. She thinks the get small word is 'papadown' or something. And she got me confused when she said the get big word is 'oopladoop'. Now I'm all mixed up. 'Oopladoop', 'hotantot', 'fatnhat'! Find me a pencil so I can write the words on my coat sleeve. I'll never get to all the children's houses if I don't get the words right."

The elf stared at Santa. "Are you going daft, Santa? You know the words as well as you know my name. ------ What is my name, anyway?" he asked, with a worried look on his face.

"Your name is Arthur, you little fussbudget. Don't try to mix me up any more. Just find me a pencil so that I can write the magic words on the sleeve of my coat. All this bother just because last year I said 'poopadoop' before I got to the bottom of the chimney at Susie's house. One little mistake and you all get the butter in a flutter."

Arthur was worried. If Santa forgot the get small word or the get big word it would be impossible to deliver all the presents before the sun came up on Christmas morning. There could not be a moment's delay. All the elves remembered how Santa said the get big word last year in Susie's chimney and got stuck. When he swelled up it made him so flustered he forgot the get small word. It was a good half hour before Santa remembered the word to get unstuck.

Arthur ran to Santa's desk to look for a pencil.

"Top drawer," Santa called out, "right next to the Good Girl -- Good Boy book."

Just then Mrs. Claus returned from the kitchen. She was carrying a steaming cup of hot chocolate. "Now, what's all the fuss?" she asked as she handed the cup of hot chocolate to Santa.

"I'm looking for a pencil," Arthur replied. "Santa wants to write the words on his coat sleeve."

"What words?" Mrs. Claus said.

"The get big word and the get small word," Arthur replied. "He is all mixed up. If he doesn't get the words right, he'll get stuck in a chimney again and never be able to finish delivering all the presents."

"For gracious sakes," said Mrs. Claus. "What's the matter with you, Santa? Are you getting feeble in the head? You know as well as I do -- the get big word is 'oopadoop' and the get small word is 'hotntot'." She paused and looked at Santa. "That's right, isn't it? 'Oopadoop' and 'hotntot'?"

"Oh, my goodness," Santa replied. "No. No. No. You are making me forget. I'll never be able to get down anyone's chimney if this keeps up. Arthur, please bring that pencil over here and stop staring at me."

Arthur had found the pencil but he was very worried. There would be big trouble if Santa forgot the words. Arthur ran to Santa.

"Careful, Arthur," Santa said. "Don't run with the pencil. You might trip and hurt yourself."

Arthur handed the pencil to Santa. "Now remember, Santa, rub your nose and say the get small word when you want to go down the chimney and don't say the get big word until you are out of the chimney and inside the house. Then when you have put the presents under the tree and you are ready to go, just rub your nose and say the get small word. Be sure you're up the chimney and into your sleigh before you say the get big word."

"O.K., O.K.," Santa said. "Please stop staring at me like I'm a nincompoop and hand me the pencil."

"You're not going to write on the sleeve of your clean coat are you, Santa?" Mrs. Claus said, with an anxious look on her face. "Pencil marks are awfully hard to remove, you know."

"Just leave them on then," Santa said. "The words will be the same next year. And please, everybody, let me think. I've got to remember the right words."

No one said anything, but both Mrs. Claus and Arthur looked worried as they watched Santa think.

"O.K.," Santa said, "the get big word is 'poopadoop' and the get small word is 'lotsasmall'." Then he wrote on the sleeve of his coat: BIG -- POOPADOOP and underneath that he wrote: SMALL -- LOTSASMALL. "There," he said, rising from his chair to head for the door.

"Wait a minute, you old puddlepuss", Mrs. Claus called out. "You forgot to kiss me good-bye. You might forget how to get back home the way you've been acting."

Santa was a head taller than Mrs. Claus, so he had to bend down to kiss his wife. He did so with much gusto, lifting her off her feet. He swung her around in a complete circle before letting her down. "Don't worry, dear. My reindeer will remember the way home, even if I forget." And out the door he went.

Santa climbed into the sleigh. It was already loaded with presents for children of every country in the world. He exclaimed to the reindeer who were chomping at the bit and eager to get on their way, "Let's go boys!" And off they went into the sky.

As the sleigh lifted into the air Santa turned to wave good-bye to Mrs. Claus and all the elves who were waving from below. As he did, he called out, "MERRY CHRIST-MAS EVERYONE and TOODLE-LEE-DOO !"

The End

THE DOLL WITH A BROKEN HEART

The first rays of dawn sparkled upon the crystals of snow as Santa and his reindeer descended from the sky early Christmas morning. They were returning to their home at the North Pole. Santa had just finished delivering Christmas presents to the homes of children around the world. It had been a long night and Santa was weary as he climbed out of his sleigh.

"Whew!" Santa said, as he stepped to the ground. "No matter how much I enjoy delivering presents it's a long trip. I sure am glad Christmas comes only once a year."

Mrs. Claus and the elves had been awaiting Santa's return. Arthur, the elf in charge of the reindeer, unhitched the reindeer from the sleigh and led them into the barn, where a meal of oats and sweet hay had been placed in their stalls. They, too, were very tired from their long trip and would fall asleep as soon as they had a bite to eat. The other elves pulled the empty sleigh into the barn by hand. They wiped away the snow so that the colorful paint and decorations on the sleigh would not be damaged by the moisture from the melting snow.

Mrs. Claus, happy to see Santa safely home, smiled a warm welcome. She held the door to the kitchen open for Santa, where she had a cup of hot chocolate awaiting his return. He dropped his cap on a kitchen chair, sat down before the crackling fire in the kitchen fireplace, and gratefully sipped the steaming beverage that was topped with a large dollop of whipped cream.

As soon as Santa finished his hot chocolate Mrs. Claus helped him pull off his boots, heavy coat, and britches. He was too tired to get into his nightshirt, so he just climbed into bed in his long red underwear. As quickly as his head settled into the pillow, he was fast asleep. Mrs. Claus pulled the covers over Santa and quietly closed the door of the bedroom. She wouldn't awaken him until the end of Christmas day after he had slept his fill.

As Mrs. Claus returned to the kitchen, the outside door suddenly burst open and two of the elves, Randolph and Franklin, ran inside the kitchen. They were carrying Santa's toy bag.

"Look, Mrs. Claus!" the elves exclaimed. "There is a present in the bottom of the bag. Santa forgot to leave one of the presents!"

"Gracious me," Mrs. Claus said. "How could that happen? Santa never forgets to leave presents for all the children."

"We think it got caught in the bottom of the bag," the elves said.

"Why that is terrible," said Mrs. Claus. "Some poor child won't receive a present. Let me see what it is."

They gathered around the kitchen table while Mrs. Claus examined the Christmas wrapping. "It says, 'TO AMANDA -- FROM SANTA', on the wrapping," she said. "Some little girl named Amanda did not receive her present. She will be brokenhearted."

Just then the package began to thump and bump and wiggle. From inside the package came the most awful sounds of a child hollering and boo-hooing. The thumping and jumping grew worse. It sounded as if a child inside the box was having a temper tantrum --- which is exactly what was happening.

"Gracious sakes alive," exclaimed Mrs. Claus, as she hurriedly tore off the Christmas wrapping. She lifted the cover of the box. There kicking its feet, wiggling and squirming and carrying on something awful, was a doll. Its face was screwed up in a most unpleasant scowl and it was howling like a banshee. No child would ever want such a disagreeable doll.

"Oh my goodness," said Mrs. Claus. "It's one of Santa's new Real-Life Dolls." Santa and the elves had invented the doll this past year. Nothing like it had ever been seen before. Each doll had been fashioned to look and act exactly like the little girl for whom it had been made. If the child who owned the doll was unhappy, the doll would be unhappy too. If the child smiled, the doll would smile too. It was magic.

Because it was a brand new creation only five Real-Life Dolls had been made. Five lucky girls would receive a Real-Life Doll under their Christmas tree this year. One child named Amanda should have been one of the lucky ones -- but Santa had not left the present under the Christmas tree at her home. It had gotten stuck in the bottom of Santa's toy bag and was never delivered.

If it had not been for the way the doll was acting, it would have been most beautiful. It had curly hair, a pretty pink dress, and silver slippers. But the dress was all wrinkled from the doll's thrashing about inside the box. A stream of tears poured from the doll's eyes, staining its cheeks and dress. It was not a pleasant sight. No one would want a doll that looked like this.

It was strange that Amanda had been chosen to receive one of the five Real-Life Dolls. The dolls were very special and were supposed to go to only the best behaved children. Even a lot of very good children would not receive a Real-Life Doll. There simply were not enough to go around. Amanda had been behaving badly ever since last Christmas. In fact, she was very spoiled and would be lucky to receive any presents at all. It was a mistake.

Amanda had written a letter to Santa two months before Christmas, during one of the few times she had been on good behavior last year. The letter was polite. She asked Santa for a very special doll. When Santa received Amanda's letter he had been busy inventing the new Real-Life Doll and scarcely had time to read the letter. Usually when he received a letter from a child asking for a present, the very first thing he did was check his Good Girl -- Good

Boy Book to see whether the child had been mostly good during the year. This time Santa forgot to look in his Good Girl -- Good Boy Book. If Santa hadn't been so busy when he opened Amanda's letter, he might have decided she shouldn't receive a present at all.

The truth was, Amanda had not been very good during the year. The year before she had received way too many presents at Christmas from her mother and father, her aunts and uncles, and even Santa. It was then that Amanda decided she must be nicer than anyone else, since she had received so many Christmas presents. She decided she deserved to have her own way, no matter how mean or nasty she was. That was when it all began, and it was not pleasant to see. Amanda became so spoiled no one wanted to be around her.

There had been occasions during the year when Amanda sassed her mother and disobeyed her father. She hadn't been nice to her little brother, and she was mean to Matilda, the family cat. The worst thing of all was Amanda's temper. If she didn't get her way she laid down on the floor, kicked her heels up and down, and yelled and cried like nothing anyone had ever seen. She found that if she yelled and screamed loud enough and rolled around on the floor making a terrible scene, her mother would give her whatever she wanted. It kept getting worse and worse, all year long. No one knew what to do.

Of course, Mrs. Claus and the elves did not know all this. The elves were aghast at the doll's behavior and stood in Mrs. Claus' kitchen staring at the crying and hollering and kicking doll. "What are we to do?" they said. "This is an awful state of affairs. Christmas is supposed to be a happy time and some little girl is screaming and hollering and crying her eyes out right this very minute."

"Well," said Mrs. Claus, "the way the doll is acting I'm surprised Amanda was supposed to receive a present. Surely Santa must have had some reason for giving such a special present to such a spoiled and ungrateful child, though I cannot imagine what it was.

"Santa may know what to do," Mrs. Claus said, "but we cannot wake him now, for it has been a long night and he needs some sleep. While he is sleeping we must figure out who was supposed to receive this doll.

"Anthony," she said to one of the elves, "will you please call all the elves into the house? We will need to work together if we are to find out who the doll was supposed to be given to."

Anthony ran outside to find the other elves. There were twenty elves all told, and some of them were napping because they had worked very hard making presents for the children.

Soon the elves began arriving into Mrs. Claus' kitchen one by one. They had worried looks about them, for Anthony had told them one little girl had not received her Christmas gift.

As the elves came into the kitchen they peered down into the box, where the doll lay crying. The doll had finally settled down a bit, but now real tears ran down the doll's cheeks, and that made the elves feel very sad. All of the elves had big hearts. Christmas was a very special time for them. All year long they worked very hard making presents.

"All right, " Mrs. Claus said, when the elves had assembled in the kitchen. "Fretting won't help. Santa didn't intend to forget any of the children. The doll simply got caught in the bottom of Santa's bag. Our job is to try to find out who the little girl is and where she lives. Santa will have to decide what to do.

"Randolph, would you please bring the Present Book from Santa's desk over here to the kitchen table? We will try to find out where the doll was supposed to go."

Randolph ran to Santa's desk. With the help of Herman, who was the strongest elf, they carried the big Present Book to the kitchen table. The elves gathered around. Some had climbed on the back of Mrs. Claus' chair and were looking over her shoulder. Some elves sat on the kitchen counter. All were thinking very hard, doing their best to help.

They opened the book to the first page. There was only one Amanda on the first page. But that Amanda could not have been the Amanda who was supposed to receive one of Santa's Real-Life Dolls. The book said this Amanda was supposed to receive a teddy bear. There were a thousand pages in the book. An hour went by as they slowly turned the pages. They were only up to the Bs. It might be several days before they found the right Amanda, much too late to repair a little girl's broken heart.

Suddenly Oliver, the elf who was the smartest and who had been peering over Mrs. Claus' shoulder as she turned the pages of the book, spoke up. "Let's have the doll look at all the Amandas in the Present Book. Maybe the doll will know where she belongs."

"That is a splendid idea, Oliver," Mrs. Claus said. She gently lifted the doll from the box and sat it in front of the Present Book. Mrs. Claus slowly turned the pages, as the doll watched. Suddenly the doll stopped crying. Mrs. Claus carefully moved her finger down the page, pointing at the names one by one. Suddenly the doll smiled.

"Stop. Stop," Oliver cried out. "The doll smiled when you pointed your finger at Amanda Washington of Wichita, Kansas. I think we may have found where the doll was supposed to be delivered."

✳ ✳ ✳ ✳ ✳ ✳ ✳ ✳ ✳ ✳ ✳ ✳

Meanwhile, in Wichita, Kansas, little Amanda Washington was sitting in a chair in front of the Christmas tree. She stared at the empty space beneath the tree, where she expected to find a beautiful doll. She felt very sorry for herself. She could not understand how Santa could possibly have forgotten her. Last year she had received a ton of presents, not only from Santa but from her father and mother and from all of her aunts and uncles too. Amanda had acted so awful to everyone. She didn't even send thank-you letters to her aunts and uncles for the presents. Her father and mother decided they would only give Amanda a sweater and a pair of winter boots this year. Amanda's aunts and uncles were so disgusted with her they gave her nothing at all. The unfortunate fact was, nobody liked her very much, because of the way she had been acting all year long.

At first, when she had run downstairs this Christmas, only to find an empty place under the tree, she had screamed and hollered. Then she lay on the floor and had a nasty temper tantrum: kicking her feet up and down, rolling from side to side, and banging her fists on the floor. Her mother felt badly for Amanda and tried to comfort her, but it did not help. She was awfully sick of Amanda's uncontrollable outbursts whenever Amanda did not get her way. Finally, Amanda's mother just walked away to let Amanda sulk.

Amanda was left alone with her head in her hands, just staring at the emptiness under the Christmas tree. She sat there for a long time. Nobody in the family paid any attention to her.

After a while Amanda began to wonder if Santa had decided not to leave a present for her on purpose because she had been so nasty all year. It hasn't been fun, having everybody mad at me, especially my mother and father and my brother. My little brother is a nice boy. I don't know why I treated him so badly. He didn't do anything to me. Even the cat doesn't like being around me.

Maybe, she thought to herself, maybe it's my own fault.

She could hear her mother and father in the kitchen doing the breakfast dishes. Amanda hadn't helped with the dishes in a long time. She walked into the kitchen and picked up a dish-towel. Much to everyone's surprise, she began drying the dishes.

Her father knew how disappointed Amanda was when she did not find a doll under the tree. Despite how nasty and thoughtless Amanda had been acting since last Christmas, her parents still loved her. "Maybe we can go to the store tomorrow and see if they have a doll like the one you wanted, Amanda. I'm afraid all the stores will be closed today, since it is Christmas. But we can go tomorrow, if that will help."

"Oh, Father," Amanda said. "Thank you, but I have been thinking. Mother works so hard washing and cleaning and cooking and taking care of us all. I can get along without a doll. Can we all go to the store and help mother pick out some things for herself?"

Amanda's parents were speechless. They stared at Amanda. This was the first time Amanda had said thank you in many months. This was the first time in a whole year she had thought about anyone else in the family beside herself.

"Did I hear correctly?" Amanda's father asked. "Did I hear you say thank you and maybe your mother might need some things for herself?"

Amanda didn't reply. She walked over to her mother and put her arms around her. Something had happened inside her that was very strange. Suddenly Amanda realized others in the family had feelings too.

✳ ✳ ✳ ✳ ✳ ✳ ✳ ✳ ✳ ✳ ✳ ✳ ✳ ✳

Santa finally woke up at four o'clock in the afternoon. He walked into the kitchen to find Mrs. Claus and the twenty elves sitting quietly. Santa was still wearing his long red underwear.

"Well, good morning," Santa said, for even though it was late in the afternoon he had only just awakened from his long sleep. "What brings all of you to the kitchen? Is it time for breakfast?" Santa smiled.

"We have been waiting for you to wake up, Santa," said Mrs. Claus. "We have a very big problem and we do not know what to do."

"Well, it must be serious. Looks like everyone is here. I would think most of you would be sound asleep. You have all been working very hard."

Mrs. Claus had been holding the doll in her lap, trying her best to comfort it. "This is a doll you and the elves made for a little girl by the name of Amanda from Witchita, Kansas. She wrote you a letter asking that you bring her a very special doll for Christmas. This is one of your Real-Life Dolls."

"Well, what is the doll doing here?" Santa asked, his brow wrinkling in concern. "The doll should have been placed under the child's tree during my rounds last night. It is not supposed to be here."

"That is the problem, Santa. Somehow the doll got caught in a fold in your toy bag and was never delivered. When the elves emptied your bag last night they found the doll."

"Jehosaphat," Santa exclaimed. "I remember the letter. Poor little girl. She so wanted a special doll of her very own. What are we to do? She must be heartbroken."

"I'm afraid so," Mrs. Claus replied. "The doll is broken-hearted too. This is one of the Real-Life Dolls. The doll and Amanda, the doll's owner, have identical feelings. Both Amanda and her doll are terribly unhappy. But we do not know what to do. You always know what to do."

"Well," Santa said, "there is only one thing we can do. I must make a second trip this very night to Witchita, Kansas. We won't need all the reindeer because we only have a single present to deliver."

Santa turned to Arthur, the elf in charge of the reindeer. "Arthur, please go out to the barn and talk to the reindeer. See which one of them is most fit to pull the small sleigh to Witchita, Kansas."

"I am sure they would all be willing to go, Santa. We told them about the mistake and they feel awful about it. Dasher is probably the strongest and most able to make the trip. I will ask him." Arthur ran out of the house to the barn.

"But, Santa," Mrs. Claus protested. "Even though you have had a few hours sleep, you must still be very tired. Are you up to another trip so soon?"

"Well, my dear. We have no other choice. There is a very sad little girl out there. We must do all we can. And we have another problem. You and the elves have discovered Amanda lives in Witchita, Kansas, but where in Witchita? There must be two dozen Amandas in Witchita. Which Amanda in Witchita does the doll belong to? How will I find Amanda's house?"

"We have been troubled about that too, Santa," Mrs. Claus replied. "We learned the doll belongs to Amanda from Witchita by holding your Present Book in front of the doll and going down the list of Amandas one by one, until the doll smiled. Then we knew that was where the doll belonged. We have put our heads together. We think, maybe, if you let the doll ride up on the seat beside you in the sleigh, she may know where she belongs. She can point to the house as you fly slowly over the city."

"Well, it will be dark soon. Let me have a little supper and after I have eaten a bit we can be on our way. Randolph," Santa said, "would you please go out to the barn and ask Arthur to hitch the small sleigh to Dasher if he is rested enough for another trip?"

Mrs. Claus made a bowl of tomato soup for Santa. She put the soup and some crackers on the kitchen table at Santa's place by the fire. "Here, Santa. Eat the soup. It will warm your bones. It's going to be cold out there tonight. There's a nip in the air. I'll get your warm clothes and hang them by the fire."

The sun had gone down and it was getting dark outside. Santa couldn't get started on his journey until after Amanda's bedtime and besides, his magic did not work until the moon came up. He broke some of the crackers into his soup. Breaking crackers into the soup may not have been the polite thing to do, but that is the way Santa liked his tomato soup. They could hear Arthur hitching Dasher to the small sleigh out in the yard.

Santa pulled on his heavy coat and britches. Mrs. Claus helped him with his boots. He found his stocking cap and pulled it down around his ears. Then he gently lifted the doll from her box and wrapped a woolen scarf around it.

Amanda had not yet named the doll, so Santa did not know what its name was. "I'm sorry I don't know your name little one," he said. "You won't have a name until Amanda names you. I'll just have to call you doll. Hope you don't mind." Of course the doll could not talk to Santa, and only Amanda would know what the doll was thinking. But Santa continued talking to the doll.

"We'll be making a fast trip to Witchita. That's where you will live. We'll need your help trying to find Amanda's house. We'll circle over the city. When we go over her house I want you to point down at it. That way we'll know which

is the right house. Be very careful. Amanda must be feeling very sad. I don't want to make another mistake by delivering you to the wrong house." Santa unbuttoned his great coat and slipped the doll inside, where it was nice and warm.

They were off. Dasher leaped into the sky and they headed for Witchita. Flying at the speed of light, it was only a few minutes before Santa and his sleigh were cruising over the city.

"Slow down a bit, Dasher," Santa called to his reindeer. "We have to let the doll get a good look at the houses." Dasher slowed to a walk. The doll peered over the side of the sleigh, looking at all the houses. Suddenly the doll pointed at one house and smiled.

"Aha!" Santa said. "I'm not surprised. I distinctly remember. I left only two presents at that house last night -- one for Amanda's little brother and one for their cat. I thought that was rather odd, since I thought there were two children and one cat living in the house. Should have been a little more careful. Haste makes waste you know."

"Down, Dasher," Santa called out to his reindeer. Dasher swooped down to land on the rooftop of the house.

Santa picked up the doll, carefully tucked her back in her box on the bed of soft tissue paper, and tied the ribbon. Then he rubbed his nose, said the magic word and zipped down the chimney. Amanda's Christmas tree was still in place. Santa carefully placed the box under the tree. He could hear giggling from inside the box. The doll was finally in its proper place and joy could once again return to Amanda's house.

In a twinkling Santa was up the chimney and into his sleigh, heading back to the North Pole.

Amanda had gone to bed that night still quite broken-hearted. She had been so sure she would receive the doll. Ever since last Christmas she always got whatever she wanted, no matter how she acted. Now, for the first time, she did not get her way. She had not liked herself much over the past year and she knew she had been awfully mean to everyone around her. As Amanda lay in bed that night real tears began to come out of her eyes -- not the crocodile tears she used when she was having a temper tantrum -- but real tears that came from a broken heart.

Amanda finally fell asleep, but not before she decided she would change her ways. When Amanda awoke in the morning, sunlight was streaming in her bedroom window. For the first time in many months she felt good about herself. She dressed and went downstairs. She walked straight to the kitchen to help her mother make breakfast for the family.

"Why, Amanda, good morning," said her mother. "You are up bright and early."

"Good morning, Mother. Can I help set the table please?"

Amanda's mother stared. "My gracious, yes. That would be a big help."

When Amanda's father and little brother sat down at the table for breakfast hardly a word was spoken. They were all afraid Amanda might have one of her temper tantrums. But that did not happen -- and would never happen again.

The witch-like spell that had surrounded Amanda for the past year was broken.

Amanda smiled and said please and thank you and felt good all over. And so did everyone else -- even Matilda, the cat. It rubbed against Amanda's leg. They both felt good.

When the dishes had been washed and put away Amanda walked into the living room, where the Christmas tree was still in place. She could not keep from looking. And there under the tree was a gift that had not been there before. She looked at the tag on the box. It said: "To Amanda from Santa". She could not believe her eyes. Was it possible she had missed the present yesterday?

She ran with the box into the kitchen. "Look, Mother. I found this under our Christmas tree. It was not there before. I am sure of it."

"Well, for goodness sake," Amanda's mother exclaimed. "Let's get the rest of the family in the living room and see what it is."

Amanda ran into the living room and called out to her little brother and to her father. They gathered around. She carefully untied the ribbon and lifted the lid of the box. Nestled in a bed of soft, white tissue paper was a beautiful doll. And it was smiling -- just like Amanda.

The End

SANTA HAS ALL THE FUN

It was a month before Christmas and the North Pole was a busy place. Although the elves had been working throughout the year making new toys for Christmas there were many things left to finish before Santa could load up his sleigh on Christmas Eve. Many of the toys needed a final coat of paint. The sleds did not have their runners attached yet. None of the toys had been wrapped and a good number of the dolls did not have any hair. A doll without hair would be a terrible thing to receive on Christmas morning.

Santa was at his big rolltop desk working on the Good Children Book when there was a knock at the door. Mrs. Claus answered the door. "Well, good morning, Homer. How are you this fine morning?" Homer was one of Santa's elves from the workshop where all the toys were made. Homer removed his hat as a courtesy to Mrs. Claus.

"Gracious me, Homer," Mrs. Claus said. "You'll catch your death of cold standing out there without your hat. Come in. Come in. Would you like a cup of hot chocolate?" she asked.

"No, thank you," Homer said, stepping inside. "I'm afraid I have to talk to Santa. We've got a bit of a problem."

Santa had overheard the conversation and came to the door. "Good morning, Homer. How are all the fellows doing in the workshop?" There were twenty elves working in the toy workshop behind Santa's house. It would be a big job finishing everything in time for Christmas.

"I'm afraid we have a problem, Santa, " Homer said with a worried look on his face. "The elves have decided they are not going to do any more work. They are sitting in the workshop doing nothing."

"Jehoshaphat! That is terrible. The toys are not finished and none of the presents have been wrapped. If the toys don't get painted soon, the paint won't dry by Christmas. Wouldn't that be awful? Wet paint on someone's clean carpet. Terrible thing. If that were to happen the mothers might decide to not have Christmas at all. What seems to be the matter?"

"The elves are complaining that they do all the work while you have all the fun."

"Well, I don't know about that. Mrs. Claus and I work pretty hard too, you know. Mrs. Claus does all the cooking for the elves. Twenty hungry mouths to feed, that's not easy. And I have to work at my desk from morning till night most of the year, keeping track of all the girls and boys in the world. Good girls and boys, and bad girls and boys too. That's no piece of chocolate cake you know.

"And what about flying around the world every Christmas Eve delivering presents, climbing up and down chimneys? I get soot in my ears and up my nose. Twice last year my bottom got singed when the fire in a fireplace was too hot. I'm about tuckered out by the time all the presents have been delivered. What about all that?" Santa exclaimed.

"Oh, yes," Homer replied. "We know you and Mrs. Claus work very hard trying to make sure children have a nice Christmas. That's not the problem. The problem is the elves think you have all the fun going into the children's homes on Christmas Eve. They never get to set foot outside the North Pole."

"Well, what about the picnic we have every summer?" Santa asked. "We have a good time when we take the day off and go up into the mountains for our annual picnic. Have they forgotten about that? It sounds to me like the elves need a good talking to," Santa said.

With that Santa pulled on his hat and coat and headed out the door to the workshop. Homer was right behind.

When Santa walked into the workshop none of the elves looked up. They were all sitting at their places by the workbench, but they were not working. They just sat, staring straight ahead. Santa could see the elves were an unhappy bunch.

"Okay, boys," Santa said. "What's the trouble? Homer tells me you're mad about something."

Pandemonium broke loose. The elves started yelling, shouting, and making a rumpus. Some jumped up from their seats and ran to Santa, pulling on his coat trying to get his attention. Three of the elves jumped up on the worktable and began shouting, "It's unfair. It's unfair!" Some of the elves hollered, "We quit! No more work!"

Santa let them carry on for a while, hoping they would get their frustration or anger -- whatever it was--out of their systems. But the elves kept getting louder and louder. Santa could see there was big trouble. Santa saw that things were going from bad to worse. "WHOA," he called out over the din. "ONE AT A TIME. NOW WHAT'S BOTHERING ALL OF YOU?"

"You tell him, Gerald," someone shouted. "Yeah, Gerald, you tell him."

The room quieted down and Gerald, the oldest elf who was almost one hundred and seventy-six years old, stepped forward.

"Well, Santa, we don't want to seem ungrateful or anything. After all, we have a nice home with you and Mrs. Claus. The food is good and our beds are always nice and tidy. You let us do the kind of work we like best, making toys for children, you know. Some of us have been helping you make toys for over a hundred years."

Santa was mystified. From what Gerald was saying, it sounded like the elves had a wonderful life. And it was true. The elves worked hard making toys, but that was what they enjoyed most. They enjoyed working with their hands. They loved making things, especially toys for children. If the elves didn't have a job like that they would just wither away with unhappiness. And they loved living at the North Pole where it was quiet and peaceful.

Two years earlier three of the elves, Freddie, Larry, and Sam, had decided they wanted to move to the city. They told Santa they were going off to make their fortune. Santa had not argued with them. He knew there was no use. Sometimes we have to find out for ourselves what the world is like. Mrs. Claus packed them good lunches and they put all their possessions in their knapsacks and headed down the road to the city.

It was a disaster. Freddie was almost run over by a truck. Larry got lost and wandered around all night with no place to sleep. Sam found a job with a sewer cleaning company. The company had been looking for someone who was small enough to climb into the sewers. They offered Sam a dollar an hour to clean the sewers. After an hour Sam handed in his resignation. It took him three days to clean up.

A week after the three adventuresome elves left to find their fortune in the city they returned to the North Pole. They were a tired, bedraggled bunch. Mrs. Claus put them to bed -- after they had taken long, hot baths and drank some of her special cranberry tonic. That was the last time any of the elves had wanted to leave their home with Santa and Mrs. Claus.

"Well, it's this way, Santa." Gerald said. "We don't mind the work. We are delighted to help load up your sleigh on Christmas Eve and wave good-bye as you head out across the heavens with the reindeer. We're glad to help make the presents for the children. The problem is, you get to see all the Christmas trees with colored lights and tinsel in the children's houses. Sometimes you get to peek in at the sleeping children. You have all the fun."

"Well, fellows," Santa said, "I appreciate how you feel. I would like to take all of you with me, but if you climbed on top after the sleigh was loaded it would be too heavy for the reindeer to lift into the sky. There is no way I can take any of you with me."

"That's O.K., Santa," Gerald said. "We know it would be too much to ask to be taken along on your trip.

"We aren't asking to go with you and we know you are very tired when you return on Christmas morning. But couldn't you stay awake just a little longer and tell us about your adventure? Tell us about the children's houses and their Christmas trees and the decorations in the villages, and maybe how children look when they sleep and are dreaming about Christmas."

"That would make all of you happy?" Santa said. "You want me to tell you what I see on my journey?"

"Yes. Yes." All the elves exclaimed together. "Please share your adventure with us so that we can enjoy it too."

Santa laughed so hard his belly shook. "Well, well, well," he replied. "Consider it done. I will tell you everything, but you have to promise me one thing."

"What's that Santa?" the elves cried out happily.

"You have to promise that all of you will stay awake while I am gone. No naps until I return on Christmas morning."

"We promise!" the elves cheered. And back to work they went, as happy as could be.

By Christmas Eve all the toys were finished and wrapped. The elves helped Santa load his sleigh for his trip around the world. As the reindeer leaped into the sky Santa called out to all the elves who were waving good-bye from the ground below, "Don't forget. No sleeping until I return."

When Santa returned on Christmas morning he remembered his promise to the elves. He went straight to the toy workshop where the elves were waiting. Of course, Santa was very tired from delivering presents and flying through the sky with the wind in his face, but a promise is a promise.

As Santa walked into the workshop the elves came running to welcome him home. True to their word, they had stayed awake all night long. Naturally they were sleepy, just as anyone would be who had been awake all night. But the excitement of hearing Santa relate his adventures would quickly wake them up.

The elves all talked at once. "What was it like, Santa? -- Tell us everything. -- Did you see the children's Christmas trees lit up with lights and pretty Christmas decorations? -- Were there stockings hung by the fireplace and a glass of milk and cookies next to the fireplace? -- Did you see any children sleeping and dreaming about finding their presents under the tree in the morning? -- Tell us! -- Tell us!"

Santa sat down in the big easy chair the elves had pulled up in front of their stone fireplace. There was a crackling fire and the room was warm and cozy. Santa sat in the easy chair and the elves sat on the floor around him, spread out all over the place. Some were sitting up and others were stretched out, resting their heads on their hands. They eagerly awaited Santa's tale.

"Well," Santa said. "First we flew down over a little village. The people had put white Christmas tree lights in all the trees up and down the main street. The light reflecting off the crystal-white snow sparkled and danced as we descended toward the first house on our list. It was dazzling and very beautiful. The reindeer stopped on the roof and I hopped off the sleigh with my bag full of Christmas presents. I laid my finger alongside my nose, said the magic word, and zipped down the chimney as neat as could be."

"And then what? Then what?" the elves eagerly exclaimed.

"There on the hearth," Santa continued, "was a glass of milk and a plate of mouth-watering brownie cookies. I drank the milk and ate all the cookies. They were delicious. Then I put the presents under the tree."

"The tree! The tree!" The elves clamoured. "Tell us about the tree. Did it have red and green and blue Christmas tree lights?"

"The tree was the most beautiful Christmas tree you ever did see," Santa replied. "It had red lights and orange lights and blue lights and purple lights and yellow lights and pink lights and violet lights and green lights. Lights of every color in the rainbow. And it had tinsel hanging from every branch. Not a single piece was out of place."

"Oh, oh, oh," the elves murmured in appreciation. "And the top of the tree. Was there an angel?"

"Oh, yes," Santa said. "The most magnificent angel you can imagine. It was dressed in silvery satin that shimmered in the lights from the tree. It sparkled and twinkled and glittered and gleamed and glowed. A magnificent angel."

"And the presents? Were there lots of presents under the tree?"

"Many Christmas presents were already under the tree when I arrived," Santa replied. "And I added the presents you fellows made. With your presents and the presents the children's parents, grandparents, and friends had placed under the tree, it was truly a wonderful sight. Some of the gifts were wrapped in Christmas paper with snowflakes and Christmas trees. Other presents were wrapped in shiny white tissue paper, and others in green and red paper. There were bows on the presents of every color -- bright red and green -- every color."

"Did you see any sleeping children dreaming about what they might find under the Christmas tree?"

"Oh, yes. At the second house the bedrooms were on the first floor, down the hall from the living room. One of the bedroom doors was open a tiny crack. I peeked in. There were two children. Their names were Jimmie and Johnnie. Each boy had his name on the foot of his bed. Both children were sound asleep. They had smiles on their faces. I think they were dreaming about what kind of presents they would get the next morning."

"Did they look happy?" the elves asked.

"Oh, yes, very happy," Santa replied. "I never saw such happy looking children. They were so happy their toes were curled."

"Toes curled?" one of the elves said. "Does being happy make children's toes curl?" The elves had never heard of happiness making your toes curl.

"Sometimes happiness makes us do funny things," Santa said. "Just like eating toast gives you curly hair."

"Did the children wake up and catch you peeking at them?"

"Oh, no," Santa said. "I am very quiet. I do not want to keep the children from getting a good night's sleep. If they don't get a good night's sleep they become cranky the next day. Being cranky on Christmas would be a very bad thing. Actually, being cranky any day is a bad thing. Nobody likes a cranky child."

Santa continued to describe what he had seen at each house. Some houses didn't have a Christmas tree at all, which made the elves very sad. A few of the houses had too many presents. Getting lots of presents seems like fun, but deep down being spoiled doesn't feel very good. Sometimes it's better to have only a few presents.

After an hour some of the elves began to get sleepy. After all, they had been up all night. Their eyelids began to get heavy, even though the stories Santa was telling were very exciting. Gradually, one by one, the elves began nodding off to sleep. They didn't want to be impolite or anything -- and they loved Santa's description of the things he had seen during his trip around the world -- but they were just too sleepy. Finally, all the elves were sound asleep. Some were sleeping sitting up and others were stretched out flat on the carpet.

When all the elves were asleep Santa quietly placed another log on the fire so that the elves would stay nice and warm. He gently covered the elves with blankets from the closet and crept quietly out the door of the toy shop.

Mrs. Claus knew about Santa's promise to the elves and was waiting for him. She helped Santa put on his night-shirt and sleeping cap. He climbed into bed. She pulled the comforter over him and before you could say 'jack rabbit' he was fast asleep.

Now it is a cherished tradition at the North Pole for Santa to share his adventures with the elves on Christmas morning. Every year when he returns home after delivering Christmas presents, he sits down before the fire with the elves at his side. There he tells the elves all the wonderful things he has seen on his journey. Every year the elves fall contentedly asleep while Santa tells them about all the happy things he saw.

Santa shares the happy things because Christmas is a time of happiness. It's full of LOVE and FUN and BEING KIND to one another. Things that elves and other little people like more than anything else.

The End

THE YOUNGEST
SHEPHERD

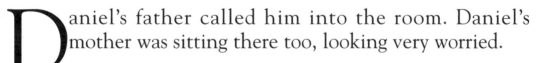

Daniel's father called him into the room. Daniel's mother was sitting there too, looking very worried.

"Son," Daniel's father said, "we must ask you to help your grandfather care for his sheep. Your grandfather is ill. He may have to come down from the mountain to the village, where he can be cared for and receive medicine from the doctors."

Although Daniel was only nine years old he had spent past summers on the mountain caring for the sheep with his grandfather. He enjoyed being with his grandfather, who had been a shepherd all his life. His grandfather was a kind and gentle man who lived in a cave on the mountain with his two sheep dogs. It was a lonely life but Daniel knew how much his grandfather loved the mountain. Daniel had grown to love it too.

During the summers they would sit together each morning, watching the sun rise above distant mountains in the east. As the sun crept higher and higher the valley below would slowly change from dusky blue to orange and then to pink. As the sun cleared the top of the mountains the whole valley would be bathed in bright sunshine, revealing groves of lush olive trees of beautiful green and gold. It was a magnificent scene that Daniel would never forget. Nor would he forget the hours of comradeship he had shared with his grandfather.

"It will not be easy," Daniel's father said. "It is September and winter comes early in the mountains. You will only have the cave for shelter. If your grandfather has to leave the mountain to seek medical care you will be on the mountain alone. You dare not leave the mountain overnight because marauding wolves are worse during the winter. You and Grandpa's dogs will have to be alert throughout the night to protect the sheep."

Grandpa's mountain was a hundred miles distant from Daniel's home. It was a four-day journey by camel. Daniel's father arranged for Daniel to join a merchant caravan carrying spices and grain to the town of Bethlehem. Bethlehem was in the valley at the foot of Grandpa's mountain. Daniel would walk the last mile up the mountain to join his grandfather.

When Daniel reached the mountainside pasture where his grandfather kept his flock of sheep, his grandfather was delighted to see him. They hugged each other warmly. Rex and Prince, grandfather's sheep dogs, came running to greet Daniel.

For the next two weeks Daniel and his grandfather shared the mountain. But Daniel could see that his grandfather was getting weaker each day from his illness. One morning as they sat together watching the dawn Daniel asked, "Grandfather how did it come that you became a sheepherder?"

"Well, my son," Grandfather replied. "I love the outdoors and I love the mountain. Many people would rather be inside. I love to be with nature. Nature is so exciting. In storms I can watch the rain marching across the valley, first to quiet the dust and then to invigorate the growing plants.

If there is thunder and lightning my blood tingles with excitement. I have never been afraid of storms but I make sure I am sheltered by the cave. Lightning seeks high things so I make sure I am not the highest thing on the mountain. I love the thunder. It is as if the gods are beating upon their drums to scare away evil."

"How did you come to this place, Grandfather?"

"I roamed many mountains seeking this particular land," grandfather replied. "Over the years I managed to save enough money to buy one hundred hectares of land. This is the best pasture anywhere. The grass is green and it is protected by hills on all sides. I have always wanted to build a house on the mountainside, where I could spend my later years and be warm and comfortable. The cave provides meager shelter against the harsh winters and it is no place to spend my later years.

"I have never been able to save enough money to build a house. Every penny of my savings has gone to purchase the land. Now that the land has finally been paid for, I had hoped to start building a sturdy stone house this very year. But I am afraid that will have to wait. My illness is getting worse. I must go to Bethlehem, where I can receive medical attention and care. I will have to leave you by yourself with my dogs and the sheep for the winter.

"I ask that you come down to Bethlehem each week bringing five sheep with you. You can leave one of the dogs with the sheep, to guard them during the day while you are off the mountain, but you will have to be back on the mountain before nightfall to protect the sheep.

"You will sell a few of the sheep each week to obtain money to pay for my medicine and care. I have one hundred sheep. If you are forced to sell five sheep each week that will provide enough money to pay for my care for twenty weeks, until the end of December. If I am not better by that time you will have to sell the land. That will break my heart, for I love the land and the mountain, but I have no other choice. I will try to get better and return as soon as I can." With those words, Daniel's grandfather bid a tearful good-bye and went down the mountain, leaving Daniel alone. Neither of them knew if he would ever return.

It was now late in December. Daniel had lived by himself on the mountain for the past four months. Each week he took five sheep down the mountain to sell in Bethlehem to raise money for his grandfather's care. His only companions on the mountain were his grandfather's sheep dogs, Rex and Prince.

Daniel's grandfather had been very sick. He was finally beginning to get better, but it would be many more months before he could regain enough strength to return to the mountain. By then there would be no sheep. There were only five sheep left. The wool from only five sheep would not be enough to support Daniel's grandfather.

Daniel could see that his grandfather would never be able to have his house on the mountainside. Soon the land would have to be sold. It seemed hopeless. Daniel had done the best he could -- but it simply was too much responsibility for someone only nine years old.

Another sheepherder from a neighboring mountain knew what had happened. He came to visit Daniel, offering to buy the land.

"Listen, boy," the man said, "you cannot make a living with only five sheep. You need a hundred sheep to make enough money from their wool to survive. You tell your grandfather, when you visit him in the village, that I will buy his land and the five sheep for twenty gold pieces. That is a very good price."

It was not a good price for the valuable land Daniel's grandfather had bought over the years; nor was it a fair price. A fair price would have been at least one hundred gold pieces. The neighbor wanted to steal the land.

Daniel told the man his grandfather would never sell the land.

The man knew he would be able to get the land when the last of the sheep were gone. He said, "I will be back in one month. Your grandfather will want to sell me the land. Then I will pay him fifteen gold pieces, and he will be happy to take it."

Daniel knew what the man said was true. No one could survive with only five sheep. The wool could only be sheared from the sheep in the spring, after the end of the winter, and that was months away. The wool from five sheep would not provide food for a month. It was a desperate time.

With only five sheep to care for Daniel did not need two sheep dogs. He did not even need one sheep dog. Two sheep dogs could guard a hundred sheep. The dogs would bring a good price, but Daniel could not bear the thought of selling Rex and Prince, for they had been Grandfather's faithful companions and were his only friends on the lonely mountainside.

Two weeks passed since the man from the neighboring mountain tried to buy the land. Daniel had thought about it a lot. There was nothing else to think about. His supplies would be exhausted soon. The land would have to be sold to the neighbor at any price, no matter how unfair.

It was almost January. Daniel could not sleep. He sat at the entrance of the cave, huddled in a blanket. Suddenly, high in the sky a brilliant star appeared in the heavens. The radiance from the star was so dazzling that the entire countryside was bathed in light. A single ray of light from the star, a star brighter than all the rest, pointed at the Inn in the town of Bethlehem. The light seemed to beckon to Daniel to follow it into town. Daniel was tempted to follow the ray but that would mean abandoning the sheep at night. He could never do that.

In the bright light from the star Daniel could see down the side of the mountain to the road at the foot of the mountain. Time passed. The star remained, casting its brilliance upon all the land. And then -- after a time -- he could make out a caravan of men and camels moving below, on the road toward the town of Bethlehem. It was unusual for anyone to be out this time of night. The caravan seemed to purposefully follow the beckoning gleam of the star. Daniel could see flags of royalty. Three men on the largest camels were dressed as kings. They wore fine robes. Guards and attendants accompanied them. Camels in the caravan carried furs and chests.

As Daniel watched the procession below one of the camels at the rear of the line suddenly kicked his hind legs and leaped into the air. Daniel saw something fly from the camel's back. As the procession continued, Daniel could see it was a chest that had been thrown off by the disobedient camel. Daniel ran to the edge of the field, calling out as loudly as he could to tell the travelers of their lost chest. They were too distant and did not hear him.

There was nothing Daniel could do. He could not leave his sheep, even for a moment, during the night.

No other travelers passed during the night. The next morning when Daniel was awakened by the sunrise, he could see the small wooden chest lying in the road, where it had dropped from the camel's back.

With the coming of daylight the threat of attack by wolves was no longer a serious danger. Putting his two sheep dogs in charge of guarding the sheep, Daniel ran down the mountainside to the road. There he found the abandoned chest.

Strong iron bands held the wooden chest together. The lid was secured by a heavy lock. Chains wrapped tightly around the chest held a second lock. Obviously the chest contained something of great value. It was the kind of chest used to transport gold from one city to another. Daniel lifted the chest. Though small, it was very heavy. It was all he could do to lift the chest to his shoulder and climb back up the mountain to his cave.

As he carefully lay the chest down, he gazed at the rich-looking adornment covering the sides of the container. He was tempted to break the locks and look inside. He had no intention of stealing the contents which, of course, belonged to the kings. But he was curious.

Maybe he could hold a gold piece in his hands. He had never held a gold piece before. Judging from how heavy the chest was, there were probably many gold pieces in the chest, and possibly some precious jewels as well. It wouldn't hurt to look, he thought.

Had he been of bad character, he could probably keep whatever was in the chest without ever being discovered. The rich travelers would not know where the chest had fallen-- and they had much more gold than they would ever need. After all, he had tried his best to call out to them. It was their fault they had not heard.

But the instant he had such thoughts Daniel scolded himself for his greed and dishonesty. He was ashamed of himself. The chest was not his to steal or to open. Somehow he must find a way to return it to its owners. He would hide it behind the rocks in his cave until he could return the chest.

Daniel could not leave his sheep to search for the leaders of the caravan in Bethlehem. He could only hope they might return along the same road. He kept a close watch.

Three days passed without a sign. The fourth day he saw a caravan heading toward him from Bethlehem. He could make out the same brightly-colored banners and decorated costumes of kings and royalty. It was daylight. The wolves would not attack. He called his dogs and instructed them to carefully guard the sheep while he descended the mountain to the road.

Daniel arrived at the road just as the first camel approached. The leader of the caravan spoke to the boy, "What do you want boy? What brings you from your sheep?"

"Oh, my Lord, four nights past I saw a caravan like yours riding toward Bethlehem. There was a very bright star in the heavens and the light was so bright it lit up the entire countryside. I do not know whether it was your caravan or not."

"Yes, son," the leader replied. "It was our caravan. We were following the star you saw to a stable in Bethlehem where a holy child was born. We took gifts to the child, who was named Jesus of Nazareth."

"Then you are the ones I saw. One of your camels acted badly and threw off a chest onto the road. I retrieved the chest and took it to my cave, awaiting your return. If you will ask your people to wait a bit, I will run to my cave to get the chest. I could not come to Bethlehem to look for you because a hungry wolf has been waiting for a chance to attack my small flock. I dared not leave them for a moment."

"Well," said the leader. "We can use a rest. We have a long way to go and the camels would like a drink of water. We will wait until you return. I will send along one of our men to help carry the chest. If it is one of our treasure chests I know it will be very heavy."

Daniel turned and began climbing the mountain. One of the guards accompanied him. When they reached the cave Daniel brought the chest to the guard, who examined it carefully. Without a word he lifted it to his shoulder to carry it down to the waiting caravan.

The guard laid the chest on the ground in front of the king. He said, "Sire, it is one of our treasure chests. It has not been opened and the chain and lock are still in place, untouched. I believe this shepherd boy is uncommonly honest and of great character."

The king spoke, "Shepherd boy, how does it happen that you are alone tending only five sheep on the side of a mountain?"

Daniel explained what had happened to his grandfather. He told the leader how he had to sell the sheep bit by bit in order to pay for the cost of medicines and care for his grandfather. Daniel told how his grandfather's hope of someday having a stone house on his beloved mountainside was no longer possible, as they were soon to lose the land to the neighbor.

The king was wise. He knew the boy could not survive for long with only five sheep. He addressed the boy once again. "The guard tells me you have not tampered with the treasure chest. You have made no attempt to examine its contents. Have you no curiosity?"

"Oh, yes, my Lord. I was most curious. The chest is very heavy and strongly constructed. I guessed it was a treasure chest, containing things of great value. I imagined it had gold and precious jewels. But it is not mine. I had no right to the chest nor even to look inside. But I must confess, I did want to look. I apologize for wanting to look."

The king and the other men laughed at that. "Well, son. There is no reason to apologize for wanting to look. Anyone would want to look. Many would want to steal the contents of the chest. We would never have found out if you had taken the chest, broken the lock and chain, and stolen the contents. I commend you for your honesty. You are a boy of great character.

"As a reward I would like you to have ten gold pieces. With ten gold pieces you can purchase supplies for yourself and care for your grandfather until he is well enough to return to the mountain."

"Oh, my Lord, I thank you. But I have done nothing to warrant such a reward. The treasure was never mine. I thank you for your kindness but I cannot take a reward for simply doing as my parents and grandfather have instructed me all my life. I am ashamed of myself for even wanting to peek in the treasure chest. I confess I wanted to hold a gold piece in my hand just to feel it. I have never held a gold piece, though I have seen one when the neighbor tried to buy my grandfather's land two weeks ago."

"And what did your neighbor offer you for your land?" the king asked.

"He offered twenty gold pieces," the boy replied. "But I know it is worth more. I told him no. He said he would be back in a month. He said he would then offer me fifteen gold pieces. I am afraid my stubbornness is going to cost my grandfather five gold pieces, as well as losing the land he loves so much."

"My son, you are not only honest and of great character, you are also wise. You will not have to sell the valuable land your grandfather worked so hard to acquire. We insist that you take the ten gold pieces."

Then one of the other kings who had been listening stepped forward. "Our young friend has proven his worth. I ask that he take the ten gold pieces you have offered and tomorrow upon our return home I will have my men come back with a hundred sheep from my flocks. I have over a thousand sheep, far too many for the size of my pasture land. It will be a service to me if the lad will take a hundred of my sheep to add to his flock."

The third king stepped forward. "I too would like to do my part. We are returning from a most awesome event. The birth of our Lord Jesus Christ. Though the child is merely an infant, we predict He will grow to become a great leader among our people. He will teach people faith and love of each other. If people can learn by His example we may have a chance to live in peace. Our troubled world is being given a new chance. This lad has shown, he too, has the honesty and strength of character to help achieve that peace.

"I wish to help him. I will have my stone masons come tomorrow to build a home on the side of the mountain. His grandfather can return to spend his remaining years in a comfortable house, to watch the sunrise each morning, and to rejoice in the splendor of life. And I wish to ask the lad to sit beside his grandfather each morning and share the joy of comradeship."

Then the first king spoke again. "You shall have all this, my son, for by your honesty you have proven your worth. Now to satisfy your curiosity, let us show you what is in the treasure chest." He took a key from a leather purse carried by a thong around his neck and hidden beneath his robes. He unlocked the lock on the chain around the chest. With a second key he unlocked the lock on the chest. He lifted the lid and dumped the contents to the ground.

Stones fell from the chest. There were no pieces of gold. There were no jewels. Daniel stared in disbelief.

The leader spoke, "You see, my son. There is nothing in the chest but worthless stones. Though the chest is disguised as a treasure chest it contains nothing of value. It is

what we call a decoy, designed to fool bandits and thieves we might encounter along our journey. It is loosely secured to the last camel in the caravan on purpose. If we are attacked, one of the guards is supposed to make the camel kick his heels to dislodge the chest, sending it flying onto the road in full view of the bandits.

"As we gallop away the thieves think we have lost a chest full of gold. They are content to let us go our way, thinking they have captured a hoard of gold. By the time they manage to break the chain and unlock the chest we are far away. We could stay behind and fight them, with possible loss of life on both sides, but we have found that using our heads instead of our swords is a better way.

"But you, young man, have learned through the teachings of your parents and your grandfather the best way of all. Honesty and good character have given your grandfather and you a fresh start in life. The pieces of gold and the sheep we will give you, and the home we will build for your grandfather is only a start, not the end. You can share this beautiful mountain with your grandfather for as long as you are willing to work.

"We followed the light of a star three nights ago to witness the birth of an infant named Jesus Christ. We hope that one day He will lead the world to a new faith. We must confess we were beginning to despair for the future, as a result of all the mean things people seem to be doing to each other.

"Today, upon meeting you in the roadway, our faith in the goodness of people is renewed. We find there are people of great honesty and good character. We thank you for renewing our belief that good character can be found in young people everywhere.

"Children are not born to be bad. Given direction by teachers, like your grandfather and your parents, children can show us they are honest and good. Your honesty in the face of strong temptation is a great gift to us.

"You may believe that the gifts we give to you this day are a blessing. We tell you that your gift to us, renewing our faith in the honesty and good character of children, is the greater blessing.

"We thank you."

As the three kings promised that day, it all came to pass. Daniel's grandfather regained his health and full strength. He returned to the mountain to find a new stone house, with a porch facing the early morning sunrise. Daniel went home in the spring to be with his father and mother,

but every summer he returns to the mountain. Each morning Daniel and his grandfather share the beauty of the blush of dawn, as the sun rises over the mountains in the east bringing new life to the valley below.

Sometimes in a summer storm, Daniel and his grandfather sit side-by-side on the porch, watching the lightning and listening with tingling excitement to the drums of thunder as they crash and echo upon the mountain. When the storm has passed, they breathe deeply of the air, cleansed and freshened by the storm.

And Daniel wondered: If others could find the peace and contentment of such moments along with the love and respect he and his grandfather shared for each other, might anger be stilled throughout the world?

The End

A Village Named Christmas

"Meeting come to order," the Mayor said as he banged the gavel on the table. "The first order of business is finding a new name for our fair city."

It wasn't really a city. It was a small town the size of a village. It was named Trash City when it was started in 1867, after its founder, Oscar Trash. In the early days villages were often named after one of their pioneers. Oscar Trash was the only citizen in the village at its beginning, so he could call it whatever he wanted. He decided he would name the village after himself. He called it Trash City.

But that was more than a hundred years ago. Oscar Trash had long since died and the village now had over eight hundred residents, including children. It was a nice place to live, but people from nearby towns sometimes said mean things like, "Oh, you are one of the trash from Trash City." Or, "Can we dump our garbage in your town - Trash City?"

It's not nice to say mean things like that and the residents of Trash City didn't like being kidded about their home town. They liked their village. They just didn't like its name. They decided it was time to give the village a new name.

"Okay," the Mayor said, "we are going to have a contest. Here are the rules. Any citizen of our community can enter the contest. Each contestant can submit one name for our town. They have one month. At the end of the month the Village Council will select the ten best names. Then the citizens will vote on those ten names. The name that gets the most votes will be the new name of our town.

"In order to stimulate a lot of interest we are going to set aside ten thousand dollars from the village budget. The citizen who comes up with the new name for our town will be allowed to spend the ten thousand dollars however he or she chooses, as long as it is for the good of the citizens of the village. For instance, buying a Civil War cannon or war monument to put in the Village Park could be a way to spend the money. Old cannons are very nice and they cost about ten thousand dollars."

Word about the contest spread quickly among the citizens of Trash City. At the end of the thirty days there were a hundred names piled up on slips of paper in front of the Mayor. Now it was up to the Village Council to select the ten names they liked best.

One of the names among the entries was Maplewood City because of the maple trees in the village. Valley View was another name, because the village was on a hill that overlooked a pretty valley. Sunrise Village seemed like a good name. Indian Hills was suggested in tribute of the Indians who had occupied the land before Oscar Trash settled there. The Village of Littlewood was a pleasant name.

One entry was Junction City for the two main roads that intersected each other in the middle of town. One citizen suggested Mill City because the village used to have a lumber mill. All were good names. Any of the names would be better than Trash City.

One name before the Village Council was a single word -- Christmas. The Mayor thought the name Christmas was silly but the other council members decided it should be one of the ten names put up for a vote.

Of the 806 citizens in the community, 252 were children. Some were only three or four years old, and a few were babies. According to the rules of the contest, every citizen was entitled to vote. That would include the children too, even though no one thought they would be interested in voting.

Mrs. Longworth was the fourth grade teacher at the local elementary school. She loved the village, and she loved the children even more. The Village Council had announced that the votes had to be in the hands of the Village Clerk by the time of the next Council meeting -- only one week away. Whichever name received the most votes would be the name of the village from that day forth, and the citizen who submitted the winning name would decide how the ten thousand dollars should be spent. The winner couldn't keep the money for himself.

Mrs. Longworth asked the school principal to hold an assembly. At the assembly slips of paper were handed out to all the children. On a blackboard were the ten names the Village Council had chosen. Every child was asked to choose one name, write it on the slip, and drop the paper through a slot in a big cardboard box. The box had been sealed tight with tape, so nobody could tamper with the votes.

Mrs. Longworth said the children would be the ones who would grow up in the village so they should have a say in what their town would be named.

On the night of the Council meeting, when the new name was to be selected, the Village Council meeting room was filled to overflowing. More people attended that meeting than any other Council meeting.

The Mayor announced, "Okay, Madam Clerk, let's count the votes."

The Village Clerk handed the Mayor a large envelope that contained pieces of paper the citizens had dropped off at the Village Hall during the week. The Mayor dumped the slips on the table and began counting. At the conclusion of the counting the Mayor announced, "Well, it looks like the winner is Maplewood City. The votes are 236 for Maplewood City. In second place is Christmas with 198 votes.

"Doesn't that beat all," the Mayor said. "I never would have believed a name like Christmas would get mor'n a couple of votes. But it makes no difference. Maplewood City wins."

Just then Mrs. Longworth stood up. "Where's the box with the children's votes?" she asked.

"Oh, that box is back in my office," the Village Clerk said. "The children don't have a vote. This is an important decision, you know."

"Aren't children citizens of this village?" Mrs. Longworth pursued.

"Well, of course they are," the Mayor replied, "but they aren't old enough to vote. You have to be a grownup to vote."

"That's not what the rules say," Mrs. Longworth replied. "You made up the rules yourself. Read the minutes of the meeting when you announced the contest."

Someone in the audience called out, "Yeah, read the rules. No one said the children aren't citizens like anyone else. Fact is, a lot of the children are better citizens than some of the adults. They have a vote too." The audience clapped loudly and some of the people cheered.

"All right. All right," the Mayor said. "Madam Clerk will you please read the minutes from the meeting a month ago, when we announced the contest?"

The Clerk opened her record book. She read from the minutes:

"The Mayor proclaimed we are going to have a contest to find a new name for our town. The Mayor announced the rules of the contest. Any citizen of our fair community can enter the contest. The contestants will submit new names for our town. They have one month. At the end of the month the Village Council will select the best ten names. Then the citizens will vote on those ten names. The name that receives the most votes wins and that will be the new name of our town. We will set aside ten thousand dollars for the contest. The winner of the contest, the citizen who comes up with the new name for our town, will be allowed to spend the ten thousand dollars however he chooses just so long as it is for the good of the citizens of the Village. The Mayor said he thought buying an old Civil War cannon or war monument to put in the Village Park would be a good project. The winner can choose whatever he wishes to spend the money on."

"Well, I guess you've got us on that one, Mrs. Longworth," the Mayor said. "The children are citizens right enough. According to the rules, they've got a vote same as anyone else. Madam Clerk, will you bring in the box with the children's votes? I've got a hunch the town's name isn't going to be Maplewood City."

The clerk hurried to her office and returned with the sealed cardboard box.

"Anybody got a knife?" the Mayor asked. "It looks like we'll have to cut the box open. They've sealed it up real good."

Someone from the audience produced a jackknife and the Mayor opened the box. The votes spilled to the table. There were 124 ballots. 119 voted in favor of Christmas.

"I guess, that settles it," the Mayor announced. "That's a total of 317 for Christmas and 198 for Maplewood City. Christmas wins by a landslide. Now, who was it that submitted the name?"

The clerk examined her records, "Well, it was Pat O'Connor, Mr. Mayor."

The Mayor peered over the top of his spectacles into the audience. It was a small town and everyone knew everyone else. "There you are Pat. Looks like your entry won the contest. You get to decide how we are going to spend the ten thousand. What do you think about a nice Civil War cannon in the Village Park?"

Pat O'Connor stood up. "Sorry, Mayor. It wasn't me who suggested the name Christmas. My suggestion was Valley View. I thought Valley View had a nice ring to it."

A few of the children were in the audience. One was Pat O'Connor's nine-year-old daughter, who was seated alongside her father. She raised her hand.

"Yes, miss," the Mayor said. "Did you want to say something? Might's well let everybody get in the act."

The girl stood up. "I think it was me," she said.

"You what?" the Mayor asked.

"I sent in the name Christmas," the girl replied. "My name is Patricia O'Connor. Everybody calls me Pat."

"You're the one who suggested we call our town Christmas? You are Pat O'Connor?"

"Yes, sir. It was me."

The entire audience cheered and clapped, showing its approval. Some of the adults patted the girl on the back. Others shook her father's hand. The other children in the audience ran from their seats to hug her.

"Well, young lady, that beats all. Not only did you win the contest, but you get to tell us how we should spend the ten thousand to commemorate our new name. I don't suppose you want us to buy a cannon for the park, do you?"

"No sir, we don't want a cannon. And we would like to talk about it in my fourth grade class at school. Can we talk about it some and come back to your next meeting to tell you how we want the money spent?"

The Mayor turned to the other Council members. "Well, folks," he said, "no reason the youngsters can't talk among themselves, is there? Young lady, you discuss it with your classmates and come back to our meeting next week. Just remember, it's got to be for the good of the citizens." Then, turning to the members of the Village Council, he said, "They'll probably want to spend all the money on some big picnic or candy or something. We'll give the kids a week and then we'll tell them how the Council has decided to spend the money."

Some people in the audience heard the Mayor's remark and didn't like it. According to the rules the winner of the contest would decide how the ten thousand would be spent, not the Village Council. It was likely the entire village would attend the next meeting to make sure the Village Council agreed to spend the money as the winner, Patricia O'Connor, and her fourth grade class decided.

In school that week Mrs. Longworth set aside an hour each day to give her class time to discuss what they would like done with the ten thousand dollars. Patricia told her classmates she would tell the Village Council to spend the money however the class voted.

The next week the entire fourth grade class attended the Village Council meeting. The room was filled to overflowing. The citizens of the community wanted to make sure the Council stuck by its promise.

"Well, young lady," the Mayor said after the meeting had begun. "Have you decided what you want us to do with the money?" The Mayor was a good politician. When he saw all the people in the audience, he knew the Council would have to honor its promise. A nine-year-old kid by the name of Patricia O'Connor was about to tell the Council how to spend ten thousand dollars. No matter what, the Council would be compelled to do as the children wished.

Patricia O'Connor stood up. She had a piece of paper in her hand. The paper stated how her fourth grade class had voted to spend the money. "First," she said, "we want to spend four hundred and thirty-five dollars on signs at both ends of town. We want the signs to say in big letters on top: CHRISTMAS. And underneath that we want the signs to say: THE FRIENDLIEST PLACE IN AMERICA.

"Mr. Johnson, the signmaker, says he will make the signs and put them up for four hundred and thirty-five dollars.

"Then we want to buy a giant Santa Claus, eight-feet high, sitting in his chair. And with a big smile. We saw a picture of it and it looks real. We want the Santa Claus to be put in the middle of the Village Park. That will cost five thousand six hundred and seventy-eight dollars. It will be delivered on a truck and put in the park, with cement underneath. We checked with the Christmas decoration store in Capitol City. The statue of Santa Claus is guaranteed to be safe from rain damage for five years, and then we can repaint it so it's just like new. Mr. Johnson said he would paint it for free when the paint washed off."

The Mayor and the members of the Village Council stared at Pat O'Connor, with their mouths open. No one said a word.

"Then we want six Santa's elves in the park, the elves who help Santa make toys. We want them peeking from behind the trees for children to discover. That will cost one thousand and forty-six dollars.

"And we want Santa to be able to talk. We asked Mr. Gillespie at the radio store. He said he could fix a radio inside the Santa Claus that will talk to people when they stand in front of him. We will turn it on at Christmas and at other times of the year when there are a lot of visitors in town. That will cost two thousand and thirty-five dollars. Mr. Gillespie said he would sign a promise to keep the radio working the way it's supposed to for five years."

The people in the audience were enthralled by the young person's recitation. Heads nodded in agreement and murmurs of approval came from all sides.

"Well," said the Mayor, "that's quite a nice project for the Village, I must say. Just what is it you want Santa Claus to say?"

"Mr. Gillespie says he can make it so that when people walk up to Santa Claus, the statue will know they are standing there and it will say things like, 'Hello. Welcome to Christmas. We are very proud of our village and we hope you enjoy your visit.'

"Then sometimes it will say, 'Hello. Welcome to our village. Christmas is the friendliest place in America. If you find anyone in town who does not say Hello you get free parking.'"

"We don't have any parking meters in town," the Mayor said. "It's all free parking."

"That's right," Patricia O'Connor replied, "and that's the way we want it to stay." The audience cheered.

"And sometimes," Patricia continued, "Santa will say, 'Welcome to Christmas. Please be nice to each other all year long.'

"There are lots of other things too. No one will ever know what Santa is going to say next, but it will always be something nice, just like at Christmas time when people are nice to each other."

"What about vandals?" the Mayor said. "What if some stranger in town decides to damage Santa Claus? That could happen, you know."

"We talked about that in school," Patricia replied. "Nobody in town would do it, but somebody from out of town might try. But we've got kids all over town. We'll watch it real good, so nobody hurts it. It's our Santa Claus. It will be a good job for us kids to look after it. We'll keep everybody responsible and catch them if they try anything funny.

"And that's the next thing. We want you to name the Village Park the Children's Park. We will take care of it, and mow the grass and keep it clean. We want it to be our responsibility."

"You say you can get all this for ten thousand?" the Mayor asked.

"Yes, sir. We talked to everybody and they agree they will do what they said. They will even sign a paper with the Village. And we still have eight hundred and six dollars left over." Patricia looked at the paper she held in her hand. "We added it all up and it comes to nine thousand one hundred and ninety-four dollars. That leaves eight hundred and six dollars. We had to get a little bit off from Mr. Johnson and Mr. Gillespie to have the money left over."

"And what do you intend to do with the eight hundred and six dollars?" the Mayor asked.

"We want you to send one dollar to everybody in town. We have eight hundred and six citizens and we want each of them to get one dollar."

"Why that's preposterous!" the Mayor exclaimed. "We never send money back to people. Where did you ever get such a crazy idea?"

"We got it from our folks," Patricia replied, not the least bothered by the Mayor's outburst. "We hear it all the time at home. Our parents say we should never give any money to the politicians because it will be wasted and we'll never see it again."

The people in the audience were dumbfounded. They would have liked to say what Patricia was saying. They simply never had the courage. Or if they had the courage, no one would listen to them.

"We can't send the money back to the people," the Mayor sputtered. "Besides who is going to pay the postage?"

"I will," said a voice in the audience. "I'll be happy to pay the postage." The voice belonged to Ray Engleman, the owner of the local hardware store. Other voices hollered, "Good for you Ray. We'll help. It's time the politicians remembered where the money comes from to begin with." Everyone in the room was laughing, slapping their legs, and playfully pounding the backs of their neighbors with great delight. Even the members of the Village Council saw the humor. They were laughing too, even the Mayor. The children had won over the entire village.

The Mayor spoke up, "Someone want to make a motion we do what Patricia O'Connor just said?"

Three members of the Village Council spoke at once. "We so move," said the Council members in unison.

"Second," said another Council member.

"All in favor?" asked the Mayor. He did not wait. "Approved unanimously," he said.

"When do we get our dollar?" shouted a voice from the audience.

"You'll get your dollar within the week," the Mayor replied, "and all the other things Patricia and her classmates have asked will be ordered tomorrow." It was a wonderful victory for the children.

Now ----- when you enter the town of Christmas you will see a big sign on the highway. On top, in big letters, it will say: CHRISTMAS. And underneath it will read: THE FRIENDLIEST PLACE IN AMERICA.

There are no parking meters anywhere in town and they never give tickets to anyone, no matter how long they stay. People say Hello, even if they have never seen you before. In the middle of town is a beautiful little park. It is called Children's Park. The grass is green and freshly mowed. The bushes are neatly trimmed and there are lots of flowers. If you walk into the park you will find an eight-foot Santa Claus with a big smile. The paint will be bright and fresh. Six elves are there, too, peeking from behind the trees hidden among the bushes. In nice weather you will see children with their parents having picnics, and mothers pushing baby carriages.

You won't see a single piece of paper in the park, anywhere. If someone drops a gum wrapper you will soon see a small child running across the grass to pick up the paper.

If you look real close you will see stones nestled in the grass and among the flowers here and there, with words cut into them. The stones say things like, "Please pause to smell the flowers" and "Please let your heart hear the singing of the birds."

Next to the small stream in the park is a stone that says: "Please enjoy the lullaby of the babbling brook." You may be lucky and find the stone that says: "Please listen to your children." You can look all over but you won't be able to find a single stone that says: "Don't."

If you visit the village around Thanksgiving and before Christmas, or in the summer when the weather's nice, you can walk up close to Santa and he will talk to you. He will say, "Hello, welcome to Christmas. Christmas is the friendliest place in all of America." Sometimes he will say, "If anyone forgets to say 'Hello' you get free parking all day long."

As you turn to walk away, Santa may call after you, "Please be nice to each other." We never know what Santa will say, but it will always be something happy and friendly.

That's the way it is in the Village of Christmas. That's the way the children wanted it.

The End

Mr. Fingle's Christmas Party

It was a pretty day, only two weeks before Christmas. Martha was walking her golden retriever on the sidewalk in front of the Bayview Convalescent Home. The Home was a block from where Martha lived. She often took her dog, whose name was Guy, for a walk in front of the Home. If the residents of the Home were sitting outside they would wave at her. But they didn't seem very happy.

It was warm outside for this time of year. Some of the residents were sitting on the front porch in the sun. Guy decided he wanted to visit. The dog walked up to one of the men on the porch and licked his hand. The man smiled and scratched the dog behind the ears. It felt good. Guy sat down.

"He won't bite," Martha said. "He likes people."

"I like him too," the man said. "We have watched you go past before when you were walking your dog. We hoped you might stop by for a visit. What's your dog's name?"

"We named him Guy. We got him when he was a puppy. He is a boy dog, so we decided to call him Guy."

"That's a nice name for a boy dog," the man said. "And what's your name?"

"My name is Martha Woods. I live in the neighborhood. My daddy's name is John Woods and my mother's name is Susan Woods. My brother's name is John Woods too, but we call him Little John. That keeps him separate from my daddy. He is five and I am seven -- pretty soon, eight. Some people call my daddy Mr. Woods."

"Well, how do you do, Martha Woods? My name is Mr. Fingle and I live here with my friends. We hope you will drop by more often, and bring Guy too."

Guy enjoyed getting his ears scratched and didn't seem to be in any hurry to leave, so Martha decided she might as well sit down too. There were other people on the porch besides Mr. Fingle. They tried to get Guy to come to where they were sitting so they could pet him. Guy looked at Martha to see if it was all right.

"That's okay, Guy. You can go see them," Martha said. "They want to pet you too."

Guy walked from one person to the next. Each one smiled at the dog and petted him. They seemed so happy to have a chance to visit with Guy. Some of the people at the Bayview Convalescent Home didn't get many visitors and they didn't smile very often. But now they were all smiling. They were happy to be petting Guy. Guy liked it too. He wagged his tail and smiled, greeting everyone on the porch.

Suddenly the door of the convalescent home burst open. A stern looking woman dressed in a starched white uniform came out on the porch. "What is going on here?" she demanded. You could tell she was angry. "What is that flea bitten mutt doing on our porch? Young lady, you have no business bringing that dog up here. Leave right now and take that dirty animal with you. It's got germs."

Martha was startled and scared. She did not like it when anybody called her dog a flea bitten mutt.

"Guy is not a flea bitten mutt. He is a very nice dog. And he is not a dirty animal, either. He just had a bath last week."

"Don't talk back to me," the attendant said in a loud voice. "I said get that dog out of here. You could infect the whole home with some disease."

"Already infected," Mr. Fingle muttered under his breath. "Infected with Miss Sourpuss' mean ways."

"I heard that," the attendant said. "Mr. Fingle, you'll be hearing from Mr. Moulton about that." Martha knew that Mr. Moulton was the administrator of the facility.

Then, shaking her finger at Martha, the woman said, "Now get that animal out of here and don't come back." She turned on her heel and stormed back into the convalescent home.

Martha ran off the porch, calling Guy to follow her. They ran home as fast as they could. Martha had liked it when Mr. Fingle and the others petted her dog. She thought they liked it too. At least they were smiling. She had never seen them smile when she walked by the home in the past. But the mean looking attendant scared her something awful. Martha knew she must have broken the law. She decided she would never go back to that place again. They might put her in jail or something.

At dinner that night Martha was quiet.

"What is the matter?" her mother asked.

At first Martha didn't say anything. She just looked down at her plate. Finally she said, "They don't like Guy."

"Who doesn't like Guy?" her father asked.

"At the Home. They told me to never come back. They said Guy was a flea bitten mutt and had germs. I felt real bad."

"You mean Bayview Convalescent Home?" Martha's father asked.

Before Martha could answer and explain what happened the telephone rang. Martha's father excused himself from the dinner table and got up to answer the phone. He talked quite a while on the phone before returning to the table.

Mr. Woods was smiling when he returned. "Well," he said with a big smile, "seems you and Guy stirred up quite a hornet's nest, Martha."

Martha knew she was in big trouble. Probably would be put in jail. She should never have let Guy go up on the porch of the convalescent home to visit with Mr. Fingle and the others.

"That was Mr. Moulton on the phone," Martha's father said. "He is the administrator of the Bayview Convalescent Home. He wants you to round up all the boys and girls in the neighborhood and their dogs and cats; and come to the Home on Saturday."

"But they told me to never come back," Martha said.

"It wasn't the Home that told you not to come back, Martha. It was one of their attendants. That was the attendant who scared you and Guy away this afternoon. The attendant quit after a little talk with Mr. Moulton today. Seems she would have been fired if she hadn't quit. They found out she was making all the people in the Home feel very sad. Any time one of them started having a little fun and feeling better she would bawl them out and make them feel badly. Mr. Moulton had been watching her. They suspected she might be the one causing a lot of problems at the Home.

"Today was the last straw. She complained that Mr. Fingle was spreading disease in the Home by inviting dogs onto the porch. What she didn't know was that Mr. Fingle donated a million dollars to Bayview two years ago, before he became unable to care for himself and had to move to Bayview. Mr. Fingle carries quite a bit a weight at the Home. When Mr. Fingle speaks, they listen."

"The woman said dogs bring germs to the Home," Martha said. "I don't want to make them sick."

"That was nonsense," Martha's father replied. "A few dogs and a cat or two are exactly what is needed over there. Mr. Moulton told me they had been planning on bringing in pets for some time. They have found that the residents are cheered up by pets. It makes them feel better to have friendly dogs and cats around to pet and hold.

"That's what the mean attendant was worried about. She doesn't like dogs, no matter how nice they are. She knew the Home was considering bringing pets in to help the residents feel better. She decided she would put a stop to it. That is why she was so mean to you and Guy. But she didn't reckon with Mr. Fingle. Mr. Fingle likes dogs -- he especially likes Guy.

"They want you and your friends to bring all the dogs and cats from the neighborhood to the care facility this Saturday. They're going to have a big celebration. They're calling it Mr. Fingle's Christmas Party. All the pets will get a piece of cake and the children will each get a Christmas present.

"Eventually they are going to let the residents have their own dogs and cats in the home to care for and to love. And on the first Saturday of every month from now on, all the children in the neighborhood are invited to bring their pets to Bayview to visit the residents, and to celebrate with a party. They have been trying to find a way to encourage children to visit. All the residents like children and wish they would visit more often. You and Mr. Fingle have shown them how to do it. From now on dogs and cats and children are welcome at the care facility -- all because of you and Mr. Fingle."

"Well, don't forget Guy," Martha said with a smile. "He helped, too."

The End

YES, VIRGINIA, THERE IS A SANTA CLAUS

A hundred years ago an eight year old girl with an inquisitive mind, encouraged by her father, wrote a letter to a New York City Newspaper, *The New York Sun.*

The girl, Virginia O'Hanlon, asked in her letter to the newspaper:

"Dear Editor,
   I am 8 years old. Some of my little friends
   say there is no Santa Claus. Papa says, 'If
   you see it in <u>The Sun</u> it's so.' Please tell me
   the truth, is there a Santa Claus?"

                    Thank you,
                    Virginia O'Hanlon

The Sun Newspaper editorial writer, Francis P. Church, was handed Virginia's letter. This is Mr. Church's reply to Virginia which appeared in the newspaper on September 21, 1897:

   VIRGINIA, your little friends are wrong.
They have been affected by the skepticism of a
skeptical age. They do not believe except they
see. They think that nothing can be which is not
comprehensible by their little minds. All minds,
Virginia, whether they be men's or children's,
are little. In this great universe of ours man is a
mere insect, an ant, in his intellect, as compared
with the boundless world about him, as mea-
sured by the intelligence capable of grasping the
whole of truth and knowledge.

   Yes, Virginia, there is a Santa Claus. He
exists as certainly as love and generosity and
devotion exist, and you know that they abound

and give to your life its highest beauty and joy. Alas! How dreary would be the world if there were no Santa Claus! It would be as dreary as if there were no Virginias. There would be no childlike faith then, no poetry, no romance to make tolerable this existence. We should have no enjoyment, except in sense and sight. The eternal light with which childhood fills the world would be extinguished.

Not believe in Santa Claus! You might as well not believe in fairies. You might get your papa to hire men to watch in all the chimneys on Christmas Eve to catch Santa Claus, but even if they did not see Santa Claus coming down, what would that prove? Nobody sees Santa Claus, but that is no sign that there is no Santa Claus. The most real things in the world are those that neither children nor men can see. Did you ever see fairies dancing on the lawn? Of course not, but that's no proof that they are not there. Nobody can conceive or imagine all the wonders there are unseen and unseeable in the world.

You tear apart the baby's rattle and see what makes the noise inside, but there is a veil covering the unseen world which not the strongest man, nor even the united strength of all the strongest men that ever lived could tear apart. Only faith, poetry, love, romance, can push aside that curtain and view and picture the supernal beauty and glory beyond. Is it all real?

Ah, Virginia, in all this world there is nothing else real and abiding.

No Santa Claus! Thank God! He lives, and lives forever. A thousand years from now, Virginia, nay, 10 times 10,000 years from now, he will continue to make glad the heart of childhood.

✳ ✳ ✳ ✳ ✳ ✳ ✳ ✳ ✳ ✳ ✳ ✳ ✳

COMMENTARY

Virginia's question began with her father. He could have ignored the question or responded in some joking fashion, treating Virginia's question as the prattle of a child. He did not. Virginia's father seized upon the opportunity to help Virginia grow into a competent, self-sufficient adult. He urged his daughter to pursue the answer to her question, to think for herself with her own letter to the editor of the newspaper. Newspapers in 1897 were the people's trusted source of truth.

The editor of the *New York Sun*, Francis P. Church, was a busy newspaper man. He could have thrown Virginia's letter in the wastebasket. He could have given her a curt 'Yes' or 'No', without further explanation. That would have been the easy thing to do.

But Mr. Church was a man sensitive to the needs and feelings of young people. He took the time to give a careful, truthful and heartfelt reply to Virginia's most serious question. A reply acknowledging that Virginia, though only eight years old, was an important person entitled to be listened to and deserving of an honest answer. He treated Virginia as an individual deserving of respect.

And what did a nurturing father and the editor's thoughtfulness achieve?

Virginia O'Hanlon Douglas grew up to become a prominent and distinquished teacher of disabled children in New York. She taught her students to have faith in themselves, to overcome their disabilities by hard work and perserverance. As a teacher, Virginia listened to the children and urged them to think for themselves, becoming responsible, self-sufficient individuals, confident of their own abilities -- just as her father and the newspaper editor had bestowed upon Virginia herself.

The result of Virginia's question to her father and, in turn to the newspaper editor, was the classic -- "Yes, Virginia, There Is A Santa Claus" -- a document which has endured for over a hundred years. Generations thereafter were thus endowed with a reason for believing. It was a gift of inestimable worth to all of us, for it is believing which opens our hearts to the spirit of love, romance and fancy. It is unyielding faith which allows us to experience the enchantment of beauty, music and poetry. Virginia's letter gave us a gift for our souls --

We do not need to see in order to believe -- we merely have to believe.

'TWAS THE NIGHT BEFORE CHRISTMAS

by Clement C. Moore

'Twas the night before Christmas,
when all through the house
Not a creature was stirring, not even a mouse;
The stockings were hung by the chimney with care,
In hopes that St. Nicholas soon would be there;
The Children were nestled all snug in their beds,
While visions of sugarplums danced in their heads;

And Mamma in her 'kerchief, and I in my cap,
Had just settled our brains for a long winter's nap;
When out on the lawn there arose such a clatter,
I sprang from the bed to see what was the matter.
Away to the window I flew like a flash,
Tore open the shutters and threw up the sash.

The moon, on the breast of the new-fallen snow,
Gave the luster of midday to objects below,
When, what to my wondering eyes should appear,
But a miniature sleigh, and eight tiny reindeer,
With a little old driver, so lively and quick,
I knew in a moment it must be St. Nick.

More rapid than eagles his coursers they came,
And he whistled, and shouted, and called them by name;
"Now, Dasher! Now, Dancer! Now, Prancer and Vixen!
On, Comet! On, Cupid! On, Donder and Blitzen!
To the top of the porch! To the top of the wall!
Now, dash away! Dash away! Dash away all!"

As dry leaves that before the wild hurricane fly,
When they meet with an obstacle, mount to the sky;
So up to the housetop the coursers they flew,
With the sleigh full of toys, and St. Nicholas, too.
And then, in a twinkling, I heard on the roof
The prancing and pawing of each little hoof ---
As I drew in my head, and was turning around,
Down the chimney St. Nicholas came with a bound.

He was dressed all in fur, from his head to his foot,
And his clothes were all tarnished with ashes and soot;
A bundle of toys he had flung on his back,
And he looked like a peddler just opening his pack.
His Eyes --- how they twinkled! His dimples, how merry!
His cheeks were like roses, his nose like a cherry!

His droll little mouth was drawn up like a bow,
And the beard of his chin was a white as the snow;
The stump of a pipe he held tight in his teeth,
And the smoke it encircled his head like a wreath;
He had a broad face and a little round belly
That shook, when he laughed, like a bowl full of jelly.

He was chubby and plump, a right jolly old elf,
And I laughed, when I saw him, in spite of myself;
A wink of his eye and a twist of his head,
Soon gave me to know I had nothing to dread;
He spoke not a word, but went straight to his work,
And filled all the stockings; then turned with a jerk,
And laying his finger aside of his nose,
And giving a nod, up the chimney he rose;
He sprang to his sleigh, to his team gave a whistle,
And away they all flew like the down of a thistle.
But I heard him exclaim, ere he drove out of sight,
"Happy Christmas to all, and to all a good night."

✳ ✳ ✳ ✳ ✳ ✳ ✳ ✳ ✳ ✳ ✳ ✳

COMMENTARY

"The Night Before Christmas," more popularly known by the first line in the poem, " 'Twas The Night Before Christmas" was first titled "An Account of a Visit from St. Nicholas."

The poem was written by Clement C. Moore to be recited from memory to his six children as they gathered around him on Christmas Eve, 1822. The children's names were Benjamin, Mary, Clement, Charity, Margaret and Emily.

Mr. Moore was the son of an Episcopal bishop. He was a noted scholar and a professor of Greek and Hebrew languages and the author of poetry and classical literature, though he is best remembered for the poem, "The Night Before Christmas."

Mr. Moore had not intended to publish the poem, but a friend wrote it down to send to *The Sentinel*, a newspaper in Troy, New York. The newspaper published the poem the next Christmas on December 23. It is from this poem that we first visualize the reindeer with their enchanting names -- Dasher, Dancer, Prancer, Vixen, Comet, Cupid, Donder and Blitzen. Rudolph did not come along until invented by another author, Robert May, in 1939 over a hundred years later.

Mr. Moore's poem also creates for generations to come an image of Santa Claus himself. The poem paints a picture of Santa as a jolly old elf with a chubby face and a round little belly which, when he laughs, shakes like a bowl full of jelly. The portrait shows a white bearded Santa with a friendly twinkle to his eyes, rosy cheeks and a bright red cherry nose. So vivid is Mr. Moore's colorful image it remains the symbol of Santa to this day. The poem is a perfect example of the powerful impact words can forge upon our imaginations. A picture in our mind which will remain for a lifetime and beyond. That should be a lesson for all of us -- be careful with our words. Words are powerful. They can motivate -- or -- they can devastate.

The End

About the Author

WILLIAM R. McTAGGART

William R. McTaggart lives near Petoskey, Michigan. He was born in Flint, Michigan in 1924, the middle child of three children. His father, David L. was a lawyer. His mother, Irene, teacher and homemaker.

Following graduation from high school in Flint he volunteered for service with the U.S. Army in 1943. A member of the Thirtieth Infantry Division, he was wounded in combat in Germany in 1944. Upon receipt of a medical discharge for his wounds, he entered the University of Michigan, graduating from law school in 1950. Upon graduation he returned to his home in Flint to join his father and younger brother, James, in the practice of law in Flint. William's older brother, David, was a medical doctor. William had four children, two of whom are surviving.

William practiced law in Flint until 1974 when he moved to a farm in northern Michigan to be able to devote more time to writing, his lifelong passion. In addition to writing, he continued his law practice in Boyne City, Michigan. In 1990 he decided to devote his life writing children's stories and established the Gramma Books Publishing Company.

❖ ❖ ❖ ❖ ❖ ❖ ❖ ❖ ❖ ❖ ❖ ❖ ❖ ❖ ❖ ❖ ❖

About the Illustrator

EUGENE J. HIBBARD

Eugene J. Hibbard, lives in Traverse City, Michigan. He was born in Chicago during the depression of the thirties. Summers were spent learning hard work on his uncle's farm in Canada.

Following graduation from high school in Detroit, Gene enlisted in the United States Air Force. He was honorably discharged in 1956. While employed at Ford Motor Co., as an industrial illustrator in Dearborn, Michigan, he attended Wayne State University in the evenings. He graduated from Wayne State with a bachelor of fine arts in advertising design.

Gene and his wife, Janet, and their three sons, moved to Traverse City in 1972 where he was employed in the Traverse City Record Eagle Newspaper advertising department as a photo/graphic specialist. He now owns and operates Hib-Art Graphic design studio in Traverse City.